The Hunt for the USS Hercules

by

Dennis Porter

TELEMACHUS PRESS

Cover designed by Telemachus Press, LLC

Cover art:
Copyright © iStockphoto 22827569tsalko
Copyright © iStockphoto 43999904_Illustration_tacktack
Copyright © iStockphoto 48866664_Illustration_esancai
Copyright © iStockphoto 61151890Illustra_Poligrafistka

Published by Telemachus Press, LLC
http://www.telemachuspress.com

Visit the author website:
http://www.dennisporter.me

ISBN: 978-1-942899-19-8 (eBook)
ISBN: 978-1-942899-20-4 (Paperback)

Version 2015.06.11

10 9 8 7 6 5 4 3 2 1

Personal Message from Dennis Porter:

I love writing books.
But what I love even more is hearing from readers.
I'm always trying to improve my writing and the way I do that is to
get
Feedback from my readers.
If you enjoyed reading this book or any of my other books
I would very much appreciate a short email
Introducing yourself.
I always personally respond to my readers.
I would very much like to put you on my mailing list to
Receive notification of future books and updates.
Let the good times roll.
http://www.dennisporter.me

Dedication

In memory of my wife, Debbie Baldwin Porter.

The Hunt for the USS Hercules

A Japanese-American Naval commander betrays his oath
The Navy's most powerful nuclear submarine
The Hercules is commandeered
Bringing *The Hercules* to the aid of Japan
As tensions between China and Japan soar
The three Gorges Dam is reduced to rubble
Nuclear missiles fly

The Hunt for the USS Hercules

Chapter 1

THERE HAD BEEN another gunfire exchange between Chinese and Filipino gunboats last night. A Chinese frigate had crossed in front of a Filipino patrol boat. The patrol boat rammed the Chinese frigate. The Chinese raked the patrol boat's deck with machine gun fire. The Filipino patrol boat responded by firing a shoulder-mounted rocket into the bridge of the Chinese frigate. There were three dead Filipino sailors, and he felt sure there were dead Chinese sailors, too. The Filipino gunboat did not want to break off the engagement.

General Mendoza lit his fortieth cigarette of the day and handed the empty pack to his orderly, who quickly disappeared to get another pack. He liked chain smoking, always had. Maybe he was smoking more—it was his nerves.

The problem was immediate and enormous in the last few months; there had been several gunfire exchanges between Filipino and Chinese gunboats. Now it was escalating. There were incidents happening almost every day, and it was becoming too combative. Trying to keep gunboat skirmishes from turning into a full-fledged battle was consuming all his time. He spent most nights begging editors not to report the fighting in the media, because an enraged public would demand action. He had told the President of the Philippines, "I do not want to get into a shooting war with China—we will lose."

There was no breeze off the Pacific. It was still hot, even though the sun had set. The night air was humid; his summer uniform stuck to him like his skin. General Mendoza, head of the Philippine military, stood with two senior generals from his staff, along with a Philippine business owner worth a few hundred million dollars. They stood waiting patiently, making small talk and casually scanning the horizon, from the secret military base thirty miles inland from the coast and twenty miles from the capital city of Manila. Deep in the jungle, the cement buildings they stood beside were windowless, and as green as the tropical forest they were designed to blend into. Finally, they heard the thump, thump of helicopter blades, as Filipino Army choppers started arriving, bringing in their guests.

General Mendoza lit another cigarette. This meeting was clandestine and the guests were arriving as covertly as conceivably possible, which all caused the general a great deal of anxiety. This base was small and only a handful of people knew of its existence. Still, it was well guarded— both physically and electronically— there would be no electronic eavesdropping. There would be six people at the meeting, and everyone had a lot to lose.

He thought about the words in the 'For Your Eyes Only' letter, hand-delivered by Rick Azar. *"Wars have a way of starting small, but quickly escalating, and then exploding out of control. In the case of the Philippines, Japan, Taiwan, and China and the American nuclear umbrella treaty, there is an enormous risk of a nuclear exchange because of a miscalculation. A nuclear exchange would destroy all our countries; it would be nothing short of devastating. I feel we are on the verge of that now. If the Chinese economy were to turn down and the government had to appease a disillusioned population, military adventurism might seem very appealing."*

He had arranged this meeting, but was unsure what to expect. The first helicopter brought in an American billionaire from the west coast; corporations he was involved with manufactured auto and truck parts, food packaging, and everything else cheap labor could produce with a price edge. These enterprises did in excess of thirty billion US dollars annually in sales, both in the United States and in the Asian Rim countries. The last to arrive was a Chinese multi-billionaire who had his tentacles in many industries. Zang Tao was known as "The Whale" for three reasons: his size of almost four hundred pounds, his wealth in billions of dollars, and his substantial influence throughout Asia. Zang Tao had quietly slipped away during a business trip inspecting garment factories in Manila. General Mendoza watched Zang Tao get out of the helicopter. "I'm glad he was the only one in that chopper; he is a load," he said to General Tazae.

They gathered in a well-guarded, clean, room, and sat down at a round table. Senior noncommissioned officers brought water, tea, and coffee, and then discreetly disappeared.

Next to their table was an enormous digital map, mounted on a board that was tilted at a slight angle. Spread across the top were three digital clocks displaying the time zones for each area of the map. Mounted in the center, below the clocks, was an electronic compass.

The map exhibited the Philippine Islands, the Spratley Islands, the Paracel Islands, the South China Sea, the Vietnam coast, Macau and Hong Kong, all of the Chinese Coast bordering on the East China Sea., The Korea Peninsula, and then all the way west to the Russian coast bordering on the Sea of Japan. The map was significant because it covered waterways China wanted to control with their newly expanded Chinese Navy.

Specifically, the focus was on three small islands that the Chinese were claiming were theirs. Of course, everyone knew the islands weren't theirs, including the Chinese. The walls of the room served as display boards. There were photos of Chinese gunboats and a battleship with a helicopter platform. There were even pictures of Chinese construction vessels pouring cement on the shore of an island, strengthening its coastline of coral reefs so Chinese vehicles could be loaded ashore.

"Thank all of you for coming. No notes or recordings of any kind are being taken. When you leave, it will be like this meeting never happened. He pointed to a large green light above the door. If any electronic eavesdropping is detected inside, or up to a half-mile outside of this room, at any time during this meeting, that light will turn red. If that happens, you need to remain quiet while I find out what is going on," General Mendoza said.

"I think all of the businessmen recognize each other. But let me do the introductions anyway: Danny Towels from America, Rick Azar, representing Philippine business interests, and lastly, Zang Tao, representing Chinese commerce. Also two members of my staff: General Bazer, who commands Philippine's Navy and Air Force, and General Tazae, who commands the Army."

General Bazer stood and pointed to a large photo.

"If the Chinese military engineers continue to reinforce the island, it will make a nice landing strip for Chinese aircraft. Additionally, it is strategically positioned and it will allow deployment of large numbers of military helicopters, which will be used to support Chinese Naval vessels. They're currently building a refueling station and aircraft hangers so they can provide air cover all the way to Australia. Additionally, it's positioned between the Philippines and American fortress at Guam."

"What they're after is control of the Philippines. At the very least a large Philippine island where they can establish a substantial force of naval vessels, fighter jets, transports, helicopters, and lots of soldiers. With the insurgency we have in the south islands, the Chinese will eventually find an island ripe for the picking. Then they will throw money and support behind some crazy rebellious group that is demanding independence," General Mendoza said. He looked at Zang Tao. Zang Tao's hands were under his chin and his eyes stared at the map where the laser pointer's red dot rested. Zang Tao noticed the pause, looked up, and nodded his head slightly.

General Tazae said, "We already have documented proof they have been supplying money and Eastern European arms into several rebellious groups on different islands. No Chinese agents have been detected to date. But it won't be long before some locals disappear and head off to Chinese political indoctrination training camps. Later others will start going to Chinese military training camps.

"It's not difficult to understand what the Chinese are after. There are vast amounts of oil and gas deposits in the South China Sea and the East China Sea. By establishing military bases on islands throughout these waters, they are attempting to claim all that oil and gas for China. It's just greed.

"Now they are trying to determine the best way to accomplish that. This is why seventy years after the end of World War Two, the Chinese are attempting to establish military outposts away from their shores. The Chinese navy wants to dominate the South Pacific region, including the Philippines, and all the way to the Australian coast."

"By having islands hundreds of miles from their coast, they can build naval bases. Thus, commercial shipping will have to pass thru the South and East China Seas that are militarily controlled by the Chinese Navy. Already we have Chinese aircraft flying over the Philippines spying on us. Currently, the Chinese fishing vessels are violating our ocean fishing boundaries; the waters of the Philippines will soon be covered with commercial Chinese fishing boats until they deplete the fish," General Mendoza said.

"With refueling and resupply bases for commercial and military naval vessels, they won't have to return to Chinese ports. They will turn the waters around the Philippines into a Chinese lake," General Bazar said.

General Bazar looked around and saw his fellow generals nodding their heads in agreement. Now, their eyes shifted to Zang Tao.

Zang Tao spoke, "What you have just described is something I was not aware of, but I suspected was happening. Although I am a business member of the Politburo, a lot of information is not given to us. But I can say in general that members of the Politburo are not in favor of military adventurism. They believe in territorial integrity and that boundaries should remain as they are. There are five members of the standing committee of the Politburo; they are not as influential as Prime Minister Li, but the council taken as a whole is more powerful than the Prime Minister.

"As one of the twenty-five Politburo members, I only have a modest amount of influence. I feel Prime Minister Li is overstepping his boundaries, but he continues to get away with it—now Li is becoming bolder. Prime Minister Li should not be making significant foreign policy decisions without consulting with the Politburo—but he does. What are his boundaries? I don't know. If the Politburo felt he acted imprudently—then he would be in an awkward position. If he loses their support—he will eventually have to step down."

"Zang Tao, are you saying Prime Minister Li is acting on his own?"

"Yes, in conjunction with heads of different ministries. I'm sure he discusses the incursions into the Philippines with his naval commanders and intelligence services. He can authorize a lot of actions but always risks undermining his office. This is especially true if he makes a risky decision that imperils China. Even more so, if he did this without the explicit authorization of the standing committee. The Politburo and the standing committee are generally very conservative."

"What are Li's intentions in the Philippines?" General Mendoza said.

"Earlier when you spoke of a military presence on some substantial island in the Philippines—I believe that is Li's intention."

"Why the Philippines?" General Bazar said.

"No real good reason; in his mind, protecting commercial shipping lanes. Perhaps the biggest reason is, Li equates a strong military that can dominate the South Pacific as China's birthright. China is the world's most populous country, our economy will soon be the largest in the world, and our military is strong. Li wants recognition; Li wants China to have its place in the sun, perhaps his own place in the sun. It is really just old thinking, nothing strategic about it." Zang Tao said.

"How can this be avoided?" General Mazda said.

"Many people in the Politburo think we are pursuing the wrong course. I sincerely believe we are treading a path of self-destruction; a path China has traveled many times in the past."

"Why is that, Zang Tao?" Danny Towels said.

"We have always had bad relations with Taiwan. But recently we have alienated Vietnam, The Philippines, Japan, Malaysian, and South Korea. In short, we are forcing countries into a group that could bond against us. If Japan armed itself with nuclear weapons and signed mutual military support treaties with the Philippines, Vietnam, South Korea, and Taiwan, that would be fortifiable opposition. Plus you have the American fortress at Guam. Perhaps then the Politburo would become involved and establish a policy that would govern the relationships with those countries."

Zang Tao looked at the American, Danny Towers.

"Danny, why does America keep involving itself in the South Pacific?"

"It's a huge mistake, perhaps a little justified after the Second World War. We had to govern Japan until they had a democracy, but after that we should have withdrawn. Truthfully, we were involved in two very expensive wars, neither of which made any sense and were a total waste of manpower and money. As a result, we are deeply in debt, and the interest we pay alone is unsustainable; there is no justification for remaining in the South Pacific. I'm in favor of withdrawing now," Danny said.

Zang Tao nodded his head in agreement. Then he clapped his hands loudly, and the room grew silent.

"Gentleman I am the one who urged Rick Azar to have General Mendoza arrange this meeting. I have specifically requested each of you because each of us will have explicit duties to perform. Duties that only you have the position and stature to execute."

He paused and leaned forward in his chair.

"Let me explain further. I want to stop China's military adventurism before we get caught up in a war. Wars have a way of starting small, but quickly escalating and then exploding out of control. In the case of the Philippines, Japan, Taiwan, and China; and the American nuclear umbrella treaty, there is an enormous risk of a nuclear exchange—because of a miscalculation. A nuclear exchange would destroy all our countries; it would be nothing short of devastating. I feel we are on the verge of that now. If the Chinese economy were to turn down and we had to confront an economic depression—coupled with high unemployment and a disillusioned population—military adventurism would seem very appealing."

General Mendoza thought—now I know whom the letter came from.

Zang Tao paused and placed both of his large hands together on the table, then carefully chose his words.

"Prime Minister Li believes China will destroy whomever we confront, quickly, with conventional forces. He forgets that the

Chinese military would have to invade over hostile oceans and open waterways that China doesn't control. I don't know what his rationale is, but he's convinced China would win these wars. I view this, as many others of the Politburo do, as very alarming. Any conflict is unproductive, but a war over three little islands with Japan and a couple in the Philippines is truly senseless."

Zang Tao stopped talking and looked at General Mendoza.

General Mendoza looked at Zang Tao with a lump in his throat and thought, he is risking everything. This big man, with enormous wealth and the world in his hands, Zang Tao, is putting all of that in jeopardy. This clandestine meeting and the words he has spoken are treasonous to Chinese ears, and for a member of the Politburo, it was incomprehensible.

Zang Tao, four hundred pounds or not—they would hang him. Confiscate his wealth, execute every member of his family, and send every relative to prison for political indoctrination, and they would never see the light of day again. They would destroy everything; every mention of his name would be stricken from the records—that is the Chinese way.

Zang Tao was staring at him. "Yes, General Mendoza, I'm going all in."

General Mendoza thought—it's like he can read my mind.

"What is your plan, Zang Tao?" General Mendoza said.

"Listen closely because it is complicated and involves a lot of risks. But it can work if well executed. Most importantly, it will prevent a political miscalculation that would lead to an enormous nuclear exchange between China and the United States. A miscalculation that would destroy our countries, our way of life, our families, and lead the world into chaos."

Then Zang Tao outlined his plan.

Chapter 2

Manila, Philippines
Two months later

GENERAL MENDOZA SAT in a clean room, inside a safe house in Manila, for his meeting with Filipino businessman Rick.

"Our intelligence service was able to purchase a Russian suitcase nuke; they had heard rumors for years that they were available on the black market.

"The service now has what we needed. It cost us a few million Euro's, but we got it. It was clandestinely purchased in Kazakhstan from a government official and a couple of high-ranking military officers. The bomb cannot be traced back to us, and that's of paramount importance."

"How much devastation will this suitcase nuke cause?" Rick asked.

"It's about four kilotons. That is equivalent to approximately one-fourth the size of the atomic bomb dropped on Hiroshima. The suitcase nukes are tactical weapons designed to destroy a large airport facility, a port facility, an Air Force base, a Naval installation, or a military base. They could take out the heart of a large city, like the financial center. They weigh just over two hundred pounds and the packaging is about three and a half feet in length and two and a half feet in width.

"The good thing about suitcase nukes is that they can't sustain a detonation beyond three to five kilotons. There's just not enough material in the case to support a larger explosion; the need to keep it portable restricts the amount of the material that can be used. So the fission is reached quickly and then there is no more material to sustain the fission."

"Why did the Russians develop a suitcase nuke?"

"Russia heard rumors that the U.S. was experimenting with miniaturizing nuclear weapons. Then Russians started experimenting with suitcase nukes during the late 1950s. The Russian General in charge of the miniaturizing of nuclear weapons chose to develop a suitcase nuke, but they never got the size reduced beyond a steamer trunk.

"Then the cold war got heated. The Russians had over two hundred suitcase nukes available. They distributed about two-thirds of the units to overseas Soviet agents. There were many suitcase nukes sent out of the Soviet Union to about fifteen countries; most of the countries were in Europe, but Japan and Korea were included. They hid the suitcase nukes inside those countries; that way they were in a position to be used if they were needed."

"Is this suitcase nuke ready to be deployed?"

"Yes; it will be completed today. We had to modernize their battery backup system. We replaced the old cell battery pack with a modern nickel-coated battery almost like in a camera. The battery backup in the steamer trunk bomb is used only to keep track of time and run the countdown to detonation. It only needs a modest amount of electrical input, but must provide that direct electrical current for a very long time. The timing mechanism has been replaced with a modern triggering and timing system of Japanese manufacturer."

"We no longer have communications between ourselves and Zang Tao. We must comply with his instructions. He is closest to the mighty of China. I'm sure everyone's communications are scrutinized, perhaps not even so discreetly," Mendoza said.

"Is the target still the same?"

"Yes. I prefer a different target, but Zang Tao inspires me; he seems so capable and so confident."

"So the target is The Three Gorges Dam?"

"Yes. I've thought about it a lot and in the end I have to agree with Zang Tao. It is a target that will embarrass the Chinese government and Prime Minister Li but is not a threat to the security of China. The Three Gorges Dam is a perfect economic target that will cripple the Chinese economy for ten to fifteen years. It produces fifteen percent of their electric power.

"Remember, it is important that this suitcase nuke is included as part of your usual shipment tomorrow, and it must not be x-rayed here. The freighter it travels on must pick up loads from at least eight ports. It's critical that the cargo be computer imaged in the Chinese port of entry." Mendoza said.

"I will make sure it is. In China, almost all industrial cargo has a computer image taken upon arrival as soon as it is unloaded. Everything passes, because you are forced to pay a bribe; that's how it is done in China. I don't think anyone looks at the computer image—may as well not even take them."

"Rick, who are you working with?"

"I will oversee the entire operation; I'm going to be hands-on all the way, until a day before the detonation. There is an old friend I grew up with and have known since the age of nine. A few years ago a small business he owned collapsed and wiped out his modest wealth. I began employing him more than a year ago; unfortunately, three months ago he was diagnosed with terminal cancer."

"Please go on," Mendoza said.

"His views parallel my opinions on the threat that China signifies to the Philippines. He has two boys and girl that are married, a son in trade school, and a daughter who is trying to get into nursing school. It's very expensive; the two in school live at home. His finances are such that he has taken a second mortgage on his home and things are very tight. His wife Milga has never worked outside the home."

"There is more?" General Mendoza said.

"A few days ago, I told him I was involved in a plot to cripple China's economy. This scheme is designed to buy desperately needed time for the Philippines to militarily enhance its capability to repulse Chinese aggression—that the mission I was involved with was a suicidal operation. His response was 'I'm a patriot. If I can make my death count, especially if I can do something for the Philippines, I will. Hopefully, this can leave my family in better financial condition.'"

"How much do you trust this man?" General Mendoza said.

"With my life, and he would do it without any financial reward. He wants to leave this world knowing he has taken care of his family. You can't blame a man for that. Can you help me with the finances?"

"More than help, and without being obvious. There is money available in our intelligence fund. His mortgage will be paid off. His daughter will attend a nursing school with all expenses paid, his son in trade school will get a job working in his tradecraft with a reliable corporation. His wife will receive a substantial sum from a post-dated life insurance policy and an attached annuity. How's that?" General Mendoza said.

"His name is Doda. Written on this note is his name, address and cell phone number. I will follow up with all the other information you will need, and will hand deliver it to you within a few days," Rick said.

"This is the perfect candidate for this job. Nothing to lose, everything to gain, and he is not associated with the Filipino military or government. Effective tomorrow, all his communications will be monitored, and he will be under twenty-four-hour surveillance. If there are any problems, you will be notified immediately."

"You won't see me again before you depart. Tomorrow at nine in the morning you will meet with the army engineer who is overseeing the mechanics of this project. He will review everything with you in detail," General Mendoza said.

"Sometimes in China things can get confused if a problem arises that will hinder the plan. I will be in contact," Rick said.

"Your communications, even in China, will be monitored. If there is a problem, say the word, 'homecoming' to the party you're talking with. We will respond within twenty-four hours."

"It's interesting that our great-grandfathers fought together against the Spanish and later the Americans in the early 1901 war for independence. Here we are today plotting against another foreign threat," Rick said.

"Lots of countries have sought control over the Philippines. I think China has always wanted to establish themselves in the Philippines, but until recently lacked the resources to achieve that goal. Now they have dusted off some ancient sea map and claim all the Spratly and Paracel islands are ancient Chinese possessions."

"If China weren't so close; it's less than eight hundred sea miles to their large Naval base at Hainan Island. If it weren't for that, I wouldn't give them a second thought," Rick said.

"Same here, but the Chinese are coming, somehow."

"We kicked out the Spanish and got rid of the Yankees and we like our independence," Rick said.

"Independence has been good for our families. We have prospered, and most of my family and relatives have done well. I have three sons serving as military officers and one son serving as a government administer in Manila. Our family has been in government service since our independence." General Mendoza said.

"Both my daughters are employed in the family business of import-export and trading all over the world. It's been a great business; the Philippines has been good to my family and me.

It is strange that our families never intermarried." Rick said.

"Not yet, anyway, but there is always hope."

They stood and shook hands. Rick walked out the door away from the safe house. General Mendoza lit the last cigarette in the pack; the pack had lasted almost till noon. He walked to the window and watched Rick walk away. It crossed his mind perhaps his great-great-grandfather had watched Rick's great-great-grandfather walking away from their meetings in the jungle, more than a hundred years ago.

Chapter 3

THE FOLLOWING MORNING, Rick went to the address he was given. It was located in downtown Manila. The building was a white and green painted, two-story cement office building with a glass double-door entrance. The advertisement mounted on the inside of the door indicated they rented business offices by the day.

He arrived a half hour early and bought coffee from a street vendor, then sat in the chair next to the vendor's stand. There are almost two million residents in Manila, and perhaps a hundred thousand street people who live in boxes, shacks, building entrances, and on the streets. He watched some of the street people searching the trash bins, moving along the streets scanning the pavement, the gutters, and the alleys, looking for anything of value.

Slowly the streets filled up with a colorful multitude of people walking everywhere—businessmen, vendors carrying cases with straps around their necks, early morning shoppers, and lots of secretaries dressed in bright clothes, with necklaces, earrings, and high heels. They were attractive and seemed business-like, but nevertheless were interesting to look at. The traffic kept his eyes moving, but it was the women who drew his attention. The coffee vendor noticed him looking at the ladies, too.

"I should have charged you more for the coffee, and double for the stool."

"You're right; this is the best seat downtown." He tipped him forty pesos.

The receptionist was expecting him and took him to a room with a large, square table and six chairs. He only had to wait a few minutes. Then a man in a plain suit entered the office. He nodded at Rick, then sat down across from him, and opened a briefcase, removing some papers with diagrams on them.

The man looked, acted, and had the bearing of a military officer. He should have just stayed in uniform; he would be more comfortable, Rick thought.

"We are not permitted to exchange names and there are no records of this meeting, nor will there ever be.

"I will give you all the technical information you need to know about the Three Gorges Dam. I will provide the most efficient method of detonation of the suitcase nuke, so the dam is entirely destroyed."

"Do you have information I can take with me?"

"Absolutely not, and no notes are to be taken! You don't want to have a diagram of the Three Gorges Dam in your possession in the event you are detained—that would be a death sentence.

"Please commit this information to memory. It won't be that difficult; that's why I made these diagrams. It simplifies the information you need to know. If you have any questions as I'm talking, interrupt me, and I will address your question. It will help you to grasp the diagram if you follow my finger as I move it along the lines of the drawing."

Rick leaned in closer and started making a mental image of the dam. His eyes following the engineer's finger as it moved slowly along the sketch lines of the massive dam.

"About the mechanics of the detonation: the water near the dam's retaining wall is approximately 540 feet deep, and the dam is approximately 7,200 feet in length. The spillway is in the center of the dam and about 1,500 feet in length; the center of the spillway is the best place for the device to detonate. There is considerable water turbulence, but the nuke is sufficiently dense to experience minimum hindrance as it makes its descent."

Rick placed a finger on the dam's spillway. "Why here?"

"It's the center of the retaining wall. There is sufficient explosive force to remove the entire dam—everything. No part of the structure will remain, and this means they will have to rebuild from scratch."

"Okay, I get it."

"The blue remote control button can be activated from a distance of a mile as long as there is a direct line of sight between the steamer trunk and the front sight of the remote. The blue button, after a ninety-second delay, will internally active the detonation mechanism. Once the detonation is activated, it cannot be stopped."

"Is a mile the maximum distance?"

"Absolutely, the closer, the better."

"Can you survive this nuke detonation from a mile away?"

"No."

The engineer and Rick looked at each other; nothing was said, but Rick got the message.

"You can depress the red button on the control; it's next to the blue button. This will immediately active the firing mechanism. There will be an immediate, small explosion and the outer casing of the steamer trunk will separate, the trapped air will escape and the suitcase nuke will lose its buoyancy. The front of the steamer trunk will start to descend first."

Rick interrupted, "How much noise from the explosion that causes the streamer trunk to start its descent?"

The engineer scratched his chin. "Because it is over water, it will sound like an oversized firecracker, followed by a muffling sound as the air escapes from the steamer trunk.

"There are exactly three-minute forty-eight seconds from the time the red button is depressed, until detonation. The nuke should be approximately eleven feet from the dam's bottom when it detonates."

"How certain are you?"

"What I described is the best scenario and will deliver the most potent blast. But as long as the nuke is one-hundred-fifty feet below the surface and within a thousand feet of the dam's retaining wall, it will destroy the dam."

"What about radiation?" Rick asked.

"This is a dirty bomb; radiation will be everywhere, but the size of a suitcase nuke will limit the contaminated area. The radiation will linger for several years, eventually losing its potency over time."

"Is the bomb completely waterproofed?"

"Yes, the unit is completely waterproofed. After it leaves the suitcase on its descent to the bottom, it is waterproofed to a depth of seven hundred feet."

"Do you have any other questions?"

"No."

"Your friend asked me to give this to you."

He reached into his briefcase and pulled out a plastic bag with two capsules in it.

"These two capsules are filled with cyanide. Each capsule contains three times the amount of cyanide needed to terminate your life. If you placed this capsule in your mouth, it would not dissolve from saliva. You could keep it in your mouth all day. If you swallowed the capsule it would pass thru your system and you could retrieve it from fecal matter and reuse it. The capsule must be crushed between your teeth. Then even a small portion of the cyanide from the capsule will be sufficient to end your life. Once the cyanide enters your system, it takes ten second to kill you."

"Have you tried that?" Rick asked.

"Tried what?"

"Swallowing a cyanide capsule and letting it pass through your system."

"No, but it has happened—it is not recommended."

The engineer looked at Rick and said, "Good luck. This meeting is over."

He stood up, placed the diagrams back in the briefcase and moved towards the entrance. He did not look back as Rick's eyes followed him out the door.

Chapter 4

A month later
Shanghai, China

RICK AND DODA sat in the Chinese version of the Range
Rover and watched the huge ocean freighters being unloaded. The
docks were frenzied with activity; it was unbelievably busy and it
made you wonder how it could even be managed. But Rick knew
every box had a destination, designated time to be there, and tons
of paperwork.

Sometime today, his containers would be unloaded, the
industrial goods inspected and x-rayed. Then the x-rays were to be
stored in computer archives. Supposedly, the x-rays would be
scanned and then stored in files. If the goods passed inspection,
then internal Chinese shipping papers would be generated. These
documents permitted the shipment to be transported within China.

It sounded official, but it was all corrupt. To get his goods
inspected in a timely fashion, he gave the shipping clerk a gratuity
that allegedly moved his goods to the front of the line. It didn't.
What it actually meant was that your cargo would not be set aside
or misplaced, or even lost. Lost meant that sometimes it would
turn up, but mostly that depended on the type of goods involved.

If they had a ready black market value, like clothing or electronics consumer goods, you could kiss them off.

If they were industrial products without an immediately available black market value, and couldn't be sold after a little time and numerous sales calls by the port thieves; then the goods would be mysteriously found and you were charged a storage fee.

Some of Rick's Chinese customers told him they had received sales calls from people in Shanghai, offering to sell his goods but at a cheaper price, and they were the same parts that they had on order from his factory. Once his company in Philippines received a call from Shanghai. The harbor thieves were trying to sell back to them the products they had just shipped to China, and at a cheaper price than the factory could manufacture them.

"If my shipment was lost, then how can you charge me a storage fee?" he once asked, out of curiosity.

"It had to be on our docks, or we wouldn't have found it—so there is a storage fee that is applied."

Sometimes doing business in China was insulting.

Rick could see the freighter his cargo had arrived on, but it was still being unloaded. Maybe his product was off, maybe it wasn't, but he didn't want to appear too anxious.

"Doda, let's get something to eat. There is a tasty rice-chicken booth at the black market. We can walk the aisles while we eat."

"Maybe we can buy some of our goods back?" Doda said.

The black market was close to eighteen blocks from the port docks and about six blocks inland from the shipping docks, towards the city center. It was convenient for the harbor thieves because they didn't have far to transport their stolen goods.

It was the largest of the black markets in Shanghai, and Rick made a point to visit here whenever he was in China, which was at least three times year. They chose fried rice and pan-fried shrimp, in cartons, that somehow tasted better than the same food in restaurants, and the price was less than an American dollar.

He found the vendor he had been looking for. He was an old man who employed a few young men. He worked the booth while the boys arranged the products. If these thieves had a specialty, it appeared to be industrial tools and pumps. He casually looked at some of the precision German automobile tools. Rick wanted to laugh; this meant that a shipment from Germany of expensive automotive tools had gotten lost in transit, which meant stolen off the dock. A sign read, "Inexpensive German automotive tools; no reasonable offers refused." They also carried industrial oil transfer pumps, industrial water pumps, dry pumps for moving grain, and centrifugal transfer pumps.

"They certainly like stealing pumps," Doda said.

"Indeed they do. This is where I purchased one of my pumps back from the shipment that was taken nineteen months ago. This is the vendor I've been looking for. Let's walk back to the Range Rover where we can talk."

In the vehicle, Rick explained what he wanted to do.

"The plan I had devised to get the pumps after they had left the Shanghai harbor was to ship them in the bulk container to our distributor in Huwan, near the three Gorges dam. Unfortunately, that leaves a paper trail.

"If we can get a couple of pumps stolen out of the shipping container at the dock, there will be an x-ray of the pumps coming into China. Then two pumps disappear without a paper trail because the port thieves have stolen them and sold them to a pump vendor at the black market. We arrange to buy the stolen pumps from the seller on the black market." Rick said.

"Then we have the suitcase nuke without a paper trail," Doda said.

"How do you know they will sell the stolen pumps to this vendor?"

"Because you're going to ask that old man at the vendor's booth for a centrifugal pump with some particular specifications, and you need two of them."

"I can order them?" Doda said.

"Not exactly. Tell him you will be in Shanghai for about five days. You will check back with him, in a few days."

"Should I give him a contact number?"

"No, nothing that can lead to us. But tell him that the pumps cost about nine thousand US dollars apiece. That you would like to buy them cheaper than that; for about five thousand US dollars cash."

"That will get his attention," Doda said.

"Doda, write this down to give to that old man. 'Centrifugal Horizontal Pump with variable speed, RPM range 2,500–4,800, self-lubricating, and aluminum construction only.' Need two pumps," Rick said.

"This afternoon when you go to give it to the vendor, first wipe your prints off the note. Then purchase some rice and chicken, then smear some chicken fat on your fingers. That way your fingerprints will be smudged in case the authorities ever get their hands on this note." Rick said.

The market stayed open until evening, but the customers thinned out after five p.m. Doda walked to the pump vendor's booth while there was still lots of pedestrian traffic moving up and down the aisles. Peering around a booth halfway down the aisle, Rick watched. Doda was talking to the old man while eating chicken and a rice ball. A few minutes later, Doda switched the chicken leg to his other hand then reached into his pocket and retrieved the note with his chicken-fat-covered fingers.

He met Doda outside the market.

"Good job. They won't get any fingerprints off that paper, just chicken grease. What did the old man say?"

"He just nodded his head until I told him that I would pay five thousand US dollars cash for each pump. Then his eyes got big and he became very attentive."

"He asked if I was interested in used pumps. I told him only new pumps. He was sure he could do something. Did I have a number that he could contact me at? I told him that I would contact him in two days' time, and I would be in Shanghai for five days." Doda said.

"Good, this end is set up."

They went back to the Gucan Park Hotel on Hutai road, just a few miles from the shipping docks. The parking lot was poorly lit, which he liked. He checked his cell phone. There was a call from the shipping clerk. He left a message: "Your shipment has arrived."

He didn't return the call from the shipping clerk. If he responded promptly and indicated he would pay a gratuity, then his shipment would be handled quickly. This time he didn't want prompt service.

They drove to the Din Ta Fung restaurant for dinner, because it was near the Jade Buddha temple. After eating, they went to the Jade Budda and chanted. Later they walked along the banks of the Huangpu River. It was a typical June night in Shanghai. The Plum rain season had begun and the temperature dropped from ninety degrees in the afternoon to around eighty at night. The high humidity made your clothes cling to your body like a second skin, and even walking left you sweaty and uncomfortable.

The next morning he had a call again from the shipping clerk. Again he didn't respond.

Instead, they took a Shanghai harbor cruise and saw ships from all over the world anchored in the harbor and the Huangpu River. The wharfs and ports operated at a frenzied pace, loading and unloading. It is a sight to behold. The river divides Shanghai into east and west. The west is the old cultural and residential center of Shanghai, and the east bank is the new financial and commercial center of the city.

They ate dinner downtown, chanted at the Jade Buddha Temple, then walked along the banks of the Huangpu River. They walked across the Nanpu suspension bridge that spanned the quarter mile over the river.

The next morning, Rick called the shipping clerk.

"Sorry, just got notified that you called. Is my shipment ready for processing?"

"I'll have to check and call you back. When you don't return my calls promptly sometimes this causes things to get misplaced. It could have even gotten lost. I will check on your shipment and call you this afternoon."

"Let me know when you find something out. Thanks."

They ate a late breakfast at the hotel. "I think our black market vendor may have the pumps you want to buy," Rick said.

They counted out two five-thousand-dollar bundles of US hundred dollar bills, then four additional stacks of one thousand dollars apiece. "I think the old man will try to drive the price up. Argue a little bit with him, but agree to it. He probably believes you were waiting for the order and it was being shipped to you, but you didn't want to pay full price so you're arranging to have it stolen off the docks to avoid paying full price."

"So he will want a higher price. Plus, he won't have to split the higher price with the port thieves, because they will never know everything is in cash," Doda said.

"Don't let the vendor bring the pumps to the car, because I don't want them to see the Range Rover or the license plate. There are laborers around the market who will load the pumps on their pushcarts and won't be suspicious. I've covered the plate with mud and won't wash it off until we get back to the hotel."

"By the time we get to the market, it will be bustling with the noonday crowd. Let's go see what the old man has for us," Doda said.

They pulled into the market. "Let's get some rice and chicken for lunch. Make sure you have lots of chicken grease on your fingers when you hand the money to the old man."

"I'm going to leave a chicken leg in the money pouch. I will wipe my fingers on it before I hand him each bundle of cash," Doda said.

They purchased fried chicken and rice balls. Rick peered around the corner of a booth and watched Doda talking to the old man. He couldn't tell what they were saying, but the old man took Doda by the arm and slowly walked him to the back of the booth.

He was pointing at something and Doda was shaking his head, no. Doda turned and began walking out of the booth. Now, the old man moved faster than he had in two days. He touched Doda's arm, said something, and Doda nodded his head.

Doda walked to the end of the aisle and motioned to one of the pushcart laborers to follow him and they walked to the vendor's booth. He pointed to the floor and the worker went to get some help.

Doda reached into his catalog pouch and handed the old man one bundle at a time. The old man slowly counted each bundle. The laborer returned with a helper and they loaded two boxes. The old man patted Doda on the back. It was a lucrative deal for him.

The two push laborers followed Doda out to the Range Rover. He popped the back lid and they slid the boxes in. He reached into his pocket and paid them with yuan. They walked away pushing the cart. Doda walked towards the market.

"What did the units look like?"

"Undamaged, like the day we boxed and shipped them, and all the same markings," Doda said.

"Why did the old man take you to the back of the booth?"

"He told me that he had to get eight thousand US for each pump, because it cost him that much to get them. He didn't want to even do this deal because there was no profit in it for him, and he only got the units for me because he had given me his word."

"Nothing like doing business in China."

"I ended up paying six thousand a pump," Doda said.

They drove back to the Gucan Park Hotel and covered the pumps with a black tarp and a strap across the top and bottom to hold them in place. They could see the Range Rover from their room windows. The car was locked and the weather was good.

It was time to call Jie, the shipping clerk, and find out the status of his shipment. Jie was unavailable and would be in a meeting for the rest of the day.

"Well, we're just going to have to hang out in Shanghai until I can get this shipment handled."

"How much time?" Doda said.

"Not sure. It's been conveniently lost so they would have enough time to sell off the two centrifugal pumps. Now they will probably wait and say they found it and pretend like nothing's missing."

"I don't like the idea of the leaving the nuke in the Ranger Rover. It is not a problem mechanically, but I worry about someone stealing the Range Rover or running into it in the parking lot."

"It's in the safest parking spot available, next to the light pole. We could disable the battery, or just sit here and watch the car," Doda said.

"I think the longest we will have to wait is a couple of days. At the latest, after the weekend on Monday."

On Monday, four days later, Rick's cell phone rang.

"Rick we found your shipment. It appears it was already sitting, waiting for your approval. When you didn't show up or contact us in a timely manner. It got moved into storage. But at least now it has been found."

"Jie, is there some way I can quickly get this shipment processed this very day, so I can get on with my business?"

"Rick, I will have to drop everything. But of course you're a good customer and a personal friend, so I will do that for you."

"Thanks, Jie, and I will make it worth your while."

He met Jie and signed the shipment for the pumps and noticed that the shipping documents had been changed to read twenty pumps instead of twenty-two pumps. He acted like he was in a hurry, and signed the shipment documents, and pretended not to notice the two missing pumps.

"Jie, can you make sure this gets trucked out today to Hydraulic Pump and Gear in Hefei?"

"Sure." Rick handed him an envelope with three hundred yuan.

"Thanks."

Rick walked out of the port gate and caught a taxi back to the hotel. Doda had their bags packed and loaded in the Range Rover, and the bill was paid.

Chapter 5

IT WAS PLUM rain season in Shanghai and the rain poured down. The long drive to Wuhan was tedious because the roads were slippery. Any sensible driver would slow down, but most Chinese with cars are first-time auto owners and inexperienced. They speed on, oblivious to slick roads as they weave in and out of traffic, and zoom past whenever the opportunity presents itself.

"The shipment is on its way to Hydraulic Pump and Gear Ltd, in Hefei?"

"It's leaving today. I gave Jie three hundred yuan to make sure it gets trucked out today. The port thieves did very well on this shipment. They steal two pumps out of the container, then we pay six thousand a piece for the pumps on the black market. Plus, they charge an extra seven hundred yuan storage fee because my shipment was lost. Actually, that was the time they needed to break into my container and steal the pumps; so they billed me for that too."

"You think that Jie gets most of that money?"

"No, I think Jie gets to keep the three hundred yuan that I gave him for a tip. The managers probably split the money from the stolen goods and dishonest storage fees. Jie knows better than to say anything, or they will fire him, or drop a container on his head."

"Nice place to work," Doda said.

"Their greed and graft worked for us. When the shipment came off the boat, it got computer imaged. They stole the pumps afterward. Now our internal Chinese shipping documents will read twenty pumps shipped to Hydraulic Pump in Hefei. The computer image will show twenty-two pumps arriving. If the authorities track down the shipment in Hefei, they will find twenty pumps. What happened to the other two pumps? They were moved out of the port without proper paperwork. That means someone was bribed, or they were stolen. And I did not report any pumps missing."

"I like Shanghai. It's a pleasant city to walk around in and there are lots of good restaurants. I liked chanting at the Jade Buddha Temple; it's so ancient. The old residential homes near the river made me feel like I was walking through the last century. The harbor boat tour and dinner were entertaining and fun, even in the rain."

"China is interesting, and Shanghai is fun. Too bad they can't keep their greedy hands off of the Philippine islands," Rick said.

"They think the Philippine Islands should belong to them."

"Why do you say that?" Rick said.

"Because they have almost one-half billion people."

"I think you're right. The Chinese with a billion and half people feel they are entitled to do whatever they want."

"That's why we have to keep the ocean between us and those cockroaches."

"This highway takes us to Wuhan. Let's check into a hotel there, because that's as close as were are going to get tonight."

"Do you have a plan on how to blow the dam?" Doda said.

"I don't know exactly. I know what I want to do, but I don't know how to do it yet."

"I would first like to get a hotel as close to the dam as possible. That way, when we blow the dam, the hotel will go with it, and any evidence that might point the Chinese authorities in our direction."

"How far from the dam can we be?"

"Maximum of a mile, perhaps a little more; depends on the terrain."

"Would downstream of the dam be best?"

"Probably."

"The problem is getting the steamer trunk into the center of the dam, then centering it in the spillway," Rick said.

"I think if we spend a couple of days walking around the dam, we'll figure something out."

"I think so too. But we can't draw any attention to ourselves."

"How much time do we have?"

"I would like to do it during Plum rain season. Then there will be a maximum amount of water washing downstream. Also, it helps to get rid of the evidence."

It was night and visibility ended ten feet past the hood of the Range Rover. The rain from the monsoon continued pounding down and its thick clouds sealed out any light from the moon. The highway was clogged and traffic moved at a snail's pace. Cars and big trucks were forced to weave in and around several accidents. When they reached Wuhan, they pulled into a travelers' motel just a few blocks off the highway.

In the morning, they ate rice, eggs, and an egg roll, with tea, for breakfast. It was still almost two hundred miles to the Three Gorges Dam. The traffic was as congested this morning as it had been last night when they drove into Wuhan.

"This place is as crowded as Shanghai," Doda said.

"It's the capital city of Hubei province and has a population of over ten million."

"Every place in China has a million people, even the little villages," Doda said.

"The way the road is congested, and with this rain, it may take us all day to get to Yichang. That's where we will stay."

"How far from the Three Gorges Dam is that?"

"About thirty miles."

The drive took all day. Finally, they reached the Three Dragons Motel, located on the outskirts of the city. It was listed as a four-star hotel, but they decided after checking in that at least two stars had to have been stolen. Its redeeming quality was that it was inconspicuous and conveniently located.

In the morning, they left the motel and drove the last thirty miles to the tourist area that overlooked the Three Gorges Dam. On the hill that overlooked the dam they could see several miles of the Yangtze on the high side of the dam. The basin with its gorges contained an enormous amount of water.

Rick recalled his meeting with the engineer, and how he moved his finger along the diagram. His finger had stopped in the middle of the dam and in the midst of the spillway, and close to the bottom of the dam. There the engineer had tapped his finger. If detonated at this point, the nuclear device will have maximum effect, and there will be nothing left of the dam or its supporting structure. It will be gone—vaporized.

The sky was overcast and it was starting to rain.

"Let's get out of here. Go back to Yichang and get some hot tea and food."

"Good. I need to take some pain pills. If I don't eat first, it makes me nauseous." Doda said.

Later that day, they sat in the room looking at the brochure of the Three Gorges Dam.

"I need to get the nuke into the center of the dam and I don't know how to do that."

"Could I load the device on a pull-along suitcase and take it on the walking tour of the dam? Get to the top of the dam and drop it over?" Doda said.

"That would be convenient, but I don't think it is going to be that easy."

"We need to take a walking tour of the dam, and a boat excursion of the dam."

"Let's take the walking tour one day and the boat trip the next day," Doda said.

He looked at Doda and realized his cancer was making him weaker every day. He had sort of forgotten about it. Doda had been taking the pain pills quietly in his own room.

"Sure, that way we can take our time and study everything thoroughly."

The next day they arranged to go on a walking tour of the Three Gorges Dam. It was an engineering marvel and its size was massive. They watched as all types of vessels moved through the five-step locks. They used their I-phones to take photos of everything. They looked for a spot where the detonation would entirely destroy the dam.

No walking across the top of the dam was permitted. You had to have special permission, something that would only be given to a film crew or foreign dignitaries. Everything you carried was subject to on-the-spot inspection.

"I don't see any way we could drop the bomb off of the top of the dam."

"I'm thinking the same thing. Plus, it weighs over two hundred pounds. I couldn't lift two hundred pounds four feet high, to get it over the guardrail, when I was healthy," Doda said.

"It would be easy enough to sneak the bomb into the ship locks. That would destroy the locks and at least half the dam."

"Probably all of Happy Village, because it's on the locks side of the Yangtze," Rick said.

"They would be vaporized like me."

"Does getting vaporized bother you?"

"Not much. What is inconvenient is this cancer that eats away at my body every day. It makes me weaker by the day. It's slowly killing me."

"Are the pain pills effective?"

"Yes, when I take enough pills, I feel no pain; none at all. I have to remind myself not to skimp on the pills. As far as my death, I've accepted my fate. I'm leaving this life and starting my journey to a new life—that is the Buddhist way."

"Tomorrow we do the boat tour."

In the morning, they boarded the Century Dragon for a day's cruise of the Three Gorges Dam, the Xiling Gorge and Yangtze. It was partly cloudy and the sun felt warm on your skin when its rays peaked through. The Yangtze was approximately a mile across as it approached the dam.

They watched mostly large, commercial vessels carrying coal, and industrial raw materials, enter the five-lock system. It took the vessels from the water level below the dam, raising them almost two hundred feet to the water level above the dam. It was time-consuming and took nearly three hours for the vessels to pass through the locks.

The larger commercial tourist boats approached the dam and got about a quarter mile away from the retaining wall. They turned and headed back upriver to Chongqing. A few of the smaller ones passed through the locks and moved on to Yichang. There were sail-driven sampans that fished in the water of the Yangtze, both above and below the dam. Generally they stayed out of the way of the commercial vessels, or navigated between them, as they sailed across the river in search of good fishing areas.

"All of the sampans had sails, but there are a few that had small outboard engines, also," Doda said.

They watched one pass beside their tour boat as they headed into the Xiling Gorge.

"That one has an electric outboard motor."

"I wonder if you can rent a sampan," Rick said.

"It would be convenient if we could rent one for fishing and sightseeing along the river," Doda said.

The boat tour had taken the entire day and had been very informative. The day's partly cloudy sky had turned to nighttime rain. They drove carefully back to Yichang and their rooms at the Three Dragon hotel.

"I need to take some pain pills, but I don't have enough with me. Let's stop by the hotel and then go out to eat. I can't take them on an empty stomach."

"Do you know why they should call it the Bad Three Dragon Hotel?" Rick said.

"No, why."

"Lousy rooms, poor cell phone reception, and horrible service."

"It should be Bad Five Dragon Hotel, terrible food and no room service," Doda said.

They ate at the Shayan a restaurant that specialized in central China cuisine. They ordered the yellow bonefish with tomato hotpot. Rick waited for Doda to finish eating and take his pain pills.

"I think we have to use the river approach to detonate the bomb. We could plant the bomb on a boat when it is waiting to enter the lock system. That would be the easiest way, but it's not the ideal location and it may not destroy the entire dam. We could plant it on a tour boat; not the one we took this morning, but one of the big cruisers. We could take the bomb on as luggage, but it doesn't come close enough to the dam."

"Unless we bribed someone to bring it closer," Doda said.

"The river police might not allow the tourist boats to get that close."

"I'm giving up my life, or what's left of it, because the future of the Philippines is at risk. I don't want the Chinese occupying our islands, and that's what they're attempting to do. They need to stay on the mainland where they belong," Doda said.

"What do you mean?"

"I want the dam to explode with maximum damage. So the message is sent is loud and clear, and unmistakable."

"Okay, I do too. What do you have in mind?"

"I think it would be best to use the sampan."

"I thought about that today. But there are some problems. First, the bomb is two hundred pounds. Second, how can you heave it out of the sampan without tipping over the sampan? Third, you have to be able to manage a sampan sail."

"I grew up in San Fernando. I sailed and fished from a sampan every day as a teenager. It was the only way our family could eat. I made a little money by selling fish. The sails I used were not the same configuration as the sails I saw being used in the sampans on the Yangtze today, but they're not much different. Let's see if we can rent one tomorrow, and test it."

"Okay, we got a week."

The next morning, the dawn brought the drizzle and they knew there would be lots of mist on the Yangtze. They purchased rain jackets in Happy Village and a fishing rod and tackle for Doda. They found the sampan boat livery recommended by the fishing tackle shop. It was located in a channel off of the Yangtze. They rented a four-person sampan, but the sampan vendor insisted that a guide had to accompany them. That doubled the cost of the rental, as the woman who rented the sampan explained: if the guide doesn't go out on the boat, he doesn't make any money.

Doda watched as the guide used the electric outboard to move the sampan into the narrow gorge. When he approached the wider expanse of the Yangtze, he expertly lashed the sails, then shut off the electric outboard and used the tiller to guide the sampan into the river.

With only a modest amount of wind on the Yangtze, the sampan moved effortlessly as it tacked back and forth across the river. The guide pointed to the far shore saying it was shallow and a good area for fishing.

Doda gave the guide fifty yuan so he could sail the sampan. Doda took the tiller with one hand, easily moving the sampan into the center of the river. He used his other hand to adjust the sail as he tacked back and forth across the Yangtze. The guide nodded his head in approval and knew that Doda had sailed a sampan before.

Doda stopped and fished along the banks, but we caught nothing. The guide used the pole and caught a yellow fish, which he kept. It was late afternoon as Doda sailed into the narrow gorge. He unlashed the sails, pushed the button that started the electric outboard and cruised the quarter mile up the channel to the sampan's dock.

As they were driving away from Happy Village and the Yangtze the, mist disappeared. But the rain began pounding down as they headed to Yichang and the Three Dragon Hotel. Doda couldn't wait, and he took some of the pain pills on an empty stomach.

"When we get to Yichang, let's go to a restaurant, have dinner, and then to the hotel."

The first restaurant they saw driving into Yichang was Wo Green Sushi. As soon as they were seated at a table, Doda ordered a rice ball and ate it quickly. He then took more pain pills with tea.

"Feel better?"

"Yes, the pills take a while before they become active. If I wait too long, the old pills wear off and the new pills haven't performed their magic yet. Then it's raw pain and it is almost unbearable."

"Can you increase your dosage?"

"I already have, but I'm going to increase it some more, I brought plenty of pain pills.

"You like the way I handled the sampan today?"

"You were as good as the guide, and that was your first time on the Yangtze."

"I know how to move the bomb to the dam. The way I would do it is come out of the boat livery using the electric outboard, then lash the sail and tack to the far side of the Yangtze. This way, I will be parallel to the dam. The vessels using the step locks will then be on the opposite side, so no interference. The wind is usually from the southwest, so it will be behind me.

"I get out of the boat in the shallow water, shove the bomb case out of the sampan and tie a rope to the case. Then, using the electric outboard, move the sampan about twenty feet in front of the dam and slowly steer the sampan parallel to the dam. When I reach the center of the spillway, I'll push the red button on the remote control. The bottom will drop out of the case.

"I will continue to use the electric motor and head towards the shore I came from—I won't get there, but it will keep my mind occupied. I will think about my family, and be happy that they are cared for. I will also be gratified that I have done my best for the Philippines," Doda said.

"I like what you just outlined. I see you have given it much thought."

"I want to do it right."

"We have to think of a way to get the suitcase nuke down the steep embankment and into the boat. It's two-hundred pounds."

"I can't say it's fishing equipment; it is too heavy."

"And we have to get rid of the guide."

"I think I can give the guide a handful of yuan not to come with me. He saw how I handled the sampan. I don't think that will be a problem."

"The day after tomorrow, we will rent the sampan for two days. The night before, we can load the suitcase nuke in the sampan after dark,like we want to get an early-morning start. Then I'll take the boat out when it begins to get light, and go directly to the dam—it's still early and no one will be around—then detonate."

"That will not work, because I need forty-eight hours to show us exiting China before the nuke is detonated."

"How can we do that?"

"Tomorrow afternoon we rent the sampan for that afternoon, and also the following three days. We'll pay in advance because we want to leave at five in the morning to fish."

The next afternoon they stopped at a sporting goods store. Afterward, they rented the same sampan and gave the guide a generous tip. He went home and still got a generous day's pay. They loaded a container of water, rice balls, and egg rolls into the sampan. Rick watched as Doda moved the sampan down the gorge towards the Yangtze.

Rick drove the Range Rover to the Yangtze where the embankment had a modest slant. He placed a rope around the suitcase nuke and let it slide slowly down the slope. He stopped it a few feet from the water's edge, then slid down the embankment, and watched as Doda rounded the bend and eased up to the embankment. A few minutes later the trunk was loaded.

Doda set the sail and tacked across the Yangtze into shallow, dark water where the fishing was good. There was no one around so they removed the wooden packing from the suitcase nuke, leaving only the waterproof casing. Standing in water, they tied the rope to a tree then placed seven twenty pound weights on top of the case.

They hung around fishing all day until it was almost dark. Doda dropped Rick at the river's edge and Rick crawled up the steep embankment as Doda rounded the bend to the boat livery. Rick met Doda and they drove towards Yichang.

"Did you need to get food to take your pain pills?"

"No, I'm not feeling any pain. We can clean up first, then go eat."

Dinner that night was at the DongPo Yuma; its cuisine was Szechuan with delicious flame-cooked, barbecue pork ribs. The restaurant sat on a hill and you could see the sampans with their lanterns aglow moving up and down the Yangtze.

He watched as Doda took several pain pills with hot tea.

"How you feeling?"

"Don't worry. I am okay. Just don't want any unnecessary pain, and I'm not worried about getting addicted to these painkillers."

"Tomorrow we check out of the hotel. I will drive you to Happy Village and you check into the Happy Hotel. I will leave you there and drive towards Hong Kong and Macau. That is a twenty-three hour drive. You should go from the motel in the morning and fish near where we stashed the suitcase nuke. Keep an eye on the location; the following day I will be in Macau."

"I thought you were flying out of Hong Kong," Doda said.

"I was, but it is possible after the dam is destroyed, the authorities may close all the Chinese airports. Macau is a Portuguese Colony and I will be able to catch Air Philippines out of there."

"When should I detonate?"

"Best time would be no later than five in the afternoon, two days from now."

"Do you want to signal me when you're safely out of the country?"

"No. There must be no communication between us unless something goes wrong; then use the code word when you speak to me."

"This is our last dinner together. We have been friends since grade school. This seems strange, having our last dinner."

"I hope, we meet again in our next lives. I promise I will look after your family and they will want for nothing."

"Thanks. This body is all done in; it's only got to last a few more days. Then it's done its job, and I won't have to take any more pain pills."

In the morning, they rose at five and checked out and headed to Happy Village, where Doda already had reservations and paid in cash. He gave his passport, credit cards and all his identification to Rick.

"Use only cash and take a taxi to the sampan rental."

"Remember to keep your cell phone with you. In case something goes terribly wrong call the emergency number. Someone will answer and they will relay the message to me. After you activate the bomb, take the battery out of your phone and throw it in the water, and then throw in your phone."

"Goodbye Doda, my friend."

"Goodbye Rick. Watch over my family."

"I promise."

Chapter 6

DODA WATCHED AS the Range Rover pulled away with Rick inside, and felt a sense of abandonment. He walked into the ground-floor room that he had rented for five days.

Doda lay on the bed and slept until almost noon. When he awoke, he wished he hadn't slept so long. He felt pain from the cancer eating his insides out, and grimaced. At least he didn't have to hide his pain from Rick anymore. He pulled a rice ball out of the bag and ate it. He took four pain pills with water. The recommended dosage was two. He didn't like pain.

He put a paperback and bottle of water in his cloth sack, then walked less than a half-mile to the sampan rental. He had reserved the sampan for a three-day. Each day the guide had to be paid a day's wages, plus a generous tip, or he pouted.

Doda pushed the button, the electric outboard purred, and he pulled into the channel. Once in the Yangtze he turned the outboard off, lashed the sail, and began to tack across the river. He liked tacking the sampan; it reminded him of his youth—so long ago—when he sailed out of San Fernando. Those were the best days of his life, only he didn't know it then.

Unlashing the sail, he steered the boat into the shallow water on the far side of the Yangtze. He adjusted his bamboo fishing hat, shading his eyes from the sun. Carefully he scanned the weeds by the trees and spotted the concealed brown twine rope that held the suitcase in place. He relaxed, and some of the guilt he felt for not being here early went away.

Sticking his fishing pole over the side, Doda sat in the back of the sampan and watched all sorts of vessels exiting the ship locks and heading upstream towards Chongqing. Doda wished he could call his wife and his children, but the call signals would later be traced when the investigation began. It would only lead to problems for them, and the Philippines. He had said his goodbyes.

Doda softly started his Buddha chant; it was relaxing and intimate, and it made him feel in touch with his soul—and forget about the cancer and its pain. He ate a rice ball and drank water and gulped down four more pain pills. The heat of the sun made him sleepy and the slight breeze sweeping across the Yangtze kept him from getting too warm, and he slept.

It was starting to get dark; he had stayed a little too long. Doda lit the lantern, then hung it from the covering pole, and with a modest wind slowly began tacking across the Yangtze. In the middle of the Yangtze it was dark; there was no moonlight. Today's sun had given way to cloud cover, and it looked like rain tonight. Tomorrow he wanted the sky filled with the sun, its rays warm upon his skin, for his last day—of this life.

Doda walked to the canteen and ordered fried rice, yellow fish, tomato hotpot and hot tea. It was a lot of food and his body needed nourishment, but the cancer diminished his appetite. He looked around at the people eating; they were local people.

They seemed to be like him, hardworking, trying to get by and raise their families. He could live next to these ordinary people. He felt sure they meant him no harm; he meant no harm to them. Doda thought about tomorrow and what would happen to these nice people—the thought didn't feel right.

It wasn't the people he was upset with; it was the government. How do things get so mixed up? He was sure the Filipino government wasn't any better than the Chinese government. All governments steal from the people, and government officials live lavishly at the ordinary man's expense. If only the Chinese would stay in their own country and keep their greedy hands off the Philippines. At least, the Filipino government didn't go around attacking people and invading their islands. Doda thought about his mission tomorrow. We are a small nation and we must fight back—the best way we can.

He went to bed but slept restlessly. He awoke several times and listened to raindrops hitting against the window. When he finally fell asleep, it was early morning.

Macau—A Portuguese Colony

Rick began the twenty-three hour drive to Macau. It was eight in the morning and he hoped to be pulling into Macau this time tomorrow.

Near midnight, he spotted a bonfire around the back side of a truck stop. Several drivers stood near the fire, keeping the chill away as they drank hot tea. He was more than halfway to Macau; he pulled around the back and parked next to the big trucks. He walked into the restaurant and bought a cup of coffee. Rick took the wood from the crates out of the Range Rover and threw them into the bonfire. He lingered discreetly in the shadows of the freight trucks, drinking coffee until the wood boxes turned to ashes.

He filled up with gas, slept for thirty minutes, and headed towards Macau. He thought about Doda and hoped he had eaten a healthy dinner, something that would give him strength and a sound night's sleep.

The super highway was a lot easier to travel at night when it was just trucks congesting the road. There were hundreds of freight vehicles moving manufactured goods to ports, and raw materials from the ports. He felt awake and on-schedule, and thought he should arrive in Macau before ten this morning.

Approaching the outskirts of Hong Kong, and less than two hours from Macau, Rick saw a truck stop displaying a billboard of a smiling tiger holding a cup of tea. He pulled into the parking area, checked the time on his cell, and set the alarm for half an hour. He pushed his seat back and slept.

Rick walked into the Smiling Tiger and stood by the door, looking around. He saw a man who looked just like Doda, gesturing with his hand to join him in his booth. It was Doda's look-alike.

Rick ordered coffee. "We're on schedule," Doda's look-alike said.

Rick slid Doda's passport and documents to the look-alike. He took the documents and examined them, then slipped the papers into his shirt pocket.

"My name is Edwardo, and I've already committed Doda's information to memory."

"How far are we from the Passport Inspection Control to get into Macau?"

"About an hour. It's best to arrive at the passport control while it is busy. Then it's almost a formality. If you're not Chinese."

When their passports were stamped, it would be documented proof that he and Doda had departed Yichang, China and entered into The Portuguese Colony of Macau.

It was almost ten as they drove across the bridge onto Macau and onto the Estrada do Istmo. Rick slowed a little and saw the sign for the Casino Venetian Macau. He pulled up to the front entrance and had the valet take his and Doda's bags. He asked the valet to hold the bags at the valet station until they checked in later today. In the hotel, he turned in the Range Rover to the Guoxin car rental.

"Yes, all is on schedule. We are flying out at ten tonight on Philippine Airlines, directly to Manila. When you check in, let the desk clerk know you just drove in from Yichang, so they remember you. I'll go down and register first. When you register, ring my room and leave a message with your number. I'm going to get some sleep," Rick said.

"I'll give you a call tonight and we'll have dinner together."

Rick slept until a little after four. He woke up and get the message that Edwardo was in room two-hundred-three; he called, and they were to meet for dinner at six.

Chapter 7

DODA FINALLY AWAKENED. He had slept later than he had yesterday. He awoke and felt the pain from the cancer. He ate a rice ball, drank water, and gulped down six pain pills. Then he rested on the bed for a half-hour before he got up, showered, and dressed. He put some rice balls and water in his cloth bag. He placed his cell phone in his pocket and walked out the door towards the sampan rental.

As he pulled the sampan into the channel, he saw the woman manager waving to him. He waved back and motored towards the Yangtze. Merging into the Yangtze, he lashed the sails and tacked across the river into the shallow waters near the far shore. It had rained all night, but this morning the sun was out and he could feel its rays on his arms. He pulled within ten feet of the hidden suitcase nuke. He saw the ropes still holding it in place.

He put his fishing pole over the side without bait. He sat there basking in the warmth of the sun and thinking of his youth in San Fernando. He thought of how he had met Milga, the way her hair hung down to her waist, the way she had smiled at him. He had loved her from the first time he saw her. She had turned and caught him staring at her, but she smiled at him. Her teeth were so white; and the delicate way she placed the vegetables in his basket, like she cared about every one of them. They would barter his fish for vegetables from her father's farm. Milga would let him get the better of the bartering because she knew his family was poor. The first time they were alone together, he had taken her fishing in his sampan, and the day had passed so quickly. They were married a year later, and had five children.

He missed her—and now he would miss her for eternity. He thought of his next life. Would he meet her—would she be willing to spend her life with him again? The sleep that had eluded him last night found him in the afternoon sun and he slept.

When he awoke, it was sundown. Doda pulled the phone from his pocket and checked the time. It was almost nine p.m. He realized that the extra pain pills he had taken had made him drowsy. He sat up but felt woozy. He steadied himself with his hand on the rail and climbed into the water of the Yangtze; its coolness sent a chill through his body. He placed his hand on his forehead; he had a fever.

It was too dark to see the brown twine rope. How could he have been so careless as to fall asleep? Their plan was no later than five p.m., almost four hours ago. He climbed back into the sampan and lit the lantern, then climbed back into the water. This time he knelt in the water and dunked his head. Its coolness cleared the grogginess from his mind.

With the light from the lantern, he found the ropes. One at a time, he removed the twenty-pound weights holding the steamer trunk under water. One dropped on his sandaled foot. He untied one line, felt the suitcase lift a little. The last line was too tight; the water had made the twine swell; it wouldn't untie. He used the fish-gutting knife to cut the rope. Slowly the suitcase nuke floated to the surface. He tied the two ropes together so it would trail about ten feet behind the sampan and not interfere with the steering. He checked his cell. It was ten p.m. The lantern could be seen for miles. He climbed into the boat and put out the light. He climbed back out and untied the sampan from the tree.

He had a mile to go, straight ahead, to reach the dam. He turned the tiller to his left to steer away from the shore. He pushed the button and the electric motor slowly got the sampan underway. He listened to the motor. It was weak, and it would never make the mile to the dam. He shut it off. He would need to use the electric outboard when he ran parallel to the dam's retaining wall where he wouldn't be able to tack back and forth.

He lashed the sails and tacked into the river, but there was only a slight wind. He began angle tacking back and forth on the river. He prayed he didn't draw attention. You were supposed to have a lantern to let other boats know your position. He only tacked to the center of the Yangtze then back, because the other shore had too much light. With a slight wind and the suitcase nuke dragging behind the sampan, it was very slow going. It took repeated efforts to turn the boat, and find the wind angle, and tack the edge.

Finally, unlashing the sails, he drifted into the corner of the retaining wall, and near the shore. He couldn't get the suitcase to trail directly behind. He now reached into his bag for the remote control for the suitcase detonator. He got out the plastic pill case. He pulled out the cell and checked the time; it was ten minutes after midnight. He was more than seven hours late.

He started the electric outboard, and slowly moved parallel to the dam and about twenty feet in front of the retaining wall. He was also close to the spillway. Suddenly, the darkness turned into daylight. The lights were blinding; he put his bamboo fishing hat on his head, but still had to turn his head down—even the light reflecting off the water hurt his eyes. A proximity sensor set to detect night movement near the dam had sensed the sampan's movement and triggered the lights on.

Doda saw flashing blue lights and sirens wailing from a large craft. It was across the Yangtze and still about a mile upstream. He was in front of the spillway but more than a hundred yards from the center. The electric motor was barely moving the sampan forward; he would never make the center before the police boat intercepted him.

He picked up the remote control detonator and depressed the red button. It was the only thing that worked as it should this night. An immediate boom sounded, and there was a flash. The nuke was released and was on its way to the bottom.

Doda knew he had less than three-minutes-forty-eight-seconds to live. He pulled out the cell phone, removed the battery, and threw it into the water, followed by the cell. The River Police had heard the boom and saw the flash of light, and it frightened them. They saw a man throw something in the water. The police boat rammed the sampan, pinning it against the retaining wall.

Doda opened the pill case and placed the cyanide pill in his mouth. A gaff hook hit him in the chest and slammed him to the floor of the sampan. Another gaffe hook pushed against his face, pinning him to the deck.

Two policemen jumped aboard. Doda bit into the cyanide pill and started his Buddhist chant. Before he could complete the first stanza, he was dead. The first policeman aboard grabbed Doda by the shirt, pulled him up and struck a hard blow to his face. Doda's head hung limp and the policeman said, "I think I killed him with one blow."

It was now ninety-three seconds to detonation.

"It's a rental sampan; maybe the old man didn't know how to sail this piece of shit."

The other policeman stood in the back, looking at the suitcase trunk still tied to the back of the boat. "What do you make of that?"

"Crazy old man was probably putting fish in it."

It was now 58 seconds to detonation.

The lieutenant boarded the sampan.

"Throw that crazy old man in the back of the sampan. I don't want him smelling up the patrol boat. We'll tie the sampan to the back of the patrol boat and tow it in. You two stay on board and get that case out of the water."

"Search his pockets."

The policeman reached in and pulled out a large handful of wet yuan.

It was now 10 seconds to detonation.

"Give me the yuan—I get half—you and the crew can split the other half."

The lieutenant took the yuan and started to count.

One, two … when a massive white light erupted from the water.

Chapter 8

AFTER DINNER, RICK and Edwardo walked into the casino. They wanted to get their faces recorded on the casino videos. It would help if the authorities started making inquiries, and it would be indisputable proof of where they had been today and tonight while they were preparing to fly out.

Rick cashed in five thousand dollars for chips at the craps table. He knew a large cash transaction would put him on the video with Doda's look-alike standing beside him. Rick idled away time by betting—a hundred on the pass line on every third row—for an hour.

The dice slowly made their way round the table and now it was Rick's turn to throw the dice. He placed some large bets on the table to be sure the videos would be recording him. He couldn't remember seeing the number twelve thrown since he had been at the table.

He placed a thousand dollar bet on number twelve. He threw the dice. The first die read six and when the second die rolled to a stop; it read six. He had thrown the number twelve. He had won thirty thousand dollars. *Now they will know where Doda and I have been tonight.*

He stood in line at the cashier's window to turn his chips into cash. He heard a voice behind him saying, "I don't like Chinese men."

He turned, and looked into the face of the most striking Chinese woman he had ever seen. Her hair was black and just brushed to her shoulders, her eyes were brown and her face had such delicate features. She was Chinese, but not Chinese—she was Eurasian.

"I don't either," Rick said.

"You're funny. My name is Mei."

"What do they call you?"

"Wealthy. But mostly Rick."

"Let's go to the lounge and get a drink," Mei said.

"Where are you from?"

"Manila, the Philippines," Rick said.

"That's where I always wanted to live."

"Really? Why?" Rick said.

"It's warm, lovely beaches and there aren't a lot of Chinese."

"You don't like Chinese?" Rick said.

"You're funny. It's complicated."

"Really?"

"Sure, when there aren't a lot of Chinese around—I'm more exotic—how's that?"

"I don't think you have a problem—of not being noticed," Rick said.

"I don't—I just like it when there are less Chinese around."

"Is that men or women?" Rick said.

"Both. Chinese men are too controlling, and Chinese women are petty, jealous, and don't like me."

"Maybe they think you are a home-wrecker."

"I don't understand—home-wrecker?" Mei said.

"It's when a man leaves his family for a mistress. Does that happen in China?"

"Every day, but it's not the Chinese way. A successful man takes a mistress, but her needs are subordinate to the wife. That is the Chinese way."

"Maybe you could get a job in Manila?" Rick said.

"I don't like to work. I had a job once; it was boring."

"How do you live?" Rick said.

"How do you think?"

"I'm not sure," Rick said.

"I find a man I like—and take good care of him."

"Lucky guy."

"You want to get lucky?" Mei said.

It was now seven in the evening as he sat having champagne in the hotel lounge with Mei, but his eyes were glued to CNN on the bar screen.

His mind was racing. The dam should have been blown this afternoon; no later than five. There should have at least been something on CNN or one of the Chinese stations. He was racking his brain. What could have gone wrong?

He had no one to talk to. Edwardo didn't know anything about the plan. He only knew he was secreted into China to pretend he was Doda—exiting China. He wished he could phone General Mendoza. He might have some information.

"You like watching the news more than talking with me?" He felt her hand on his thigh.

"No, it just a business habit. Staying on top of the news."

"I have to find my friend Doda and talk a little business with him. Can you go to your room and I will meet you there? We'll order room service and chat."

"I like that. How much time?"

"About an hour."

He pulled Edwardo away from the slots.

"Something has come up. I want you to stay on the ten p.m. flight tonight. I will catch a later flight tonight, or the first thing in the morning. But no later than that."

"That beautiful Chinese girl got you distracted?"

He liked that Edwardo thought that—so probably people watching a video would, too.

"Wouldn't you get distracted?"

"See you back in Manila."

He sat in the lounge and thought. *If Doda knew he was going to get caught, he would take the cyanide pill. What if someone found the nuke device? It would take a while, and a good scientist, to figure out what it was. What if Doda died from the cancer in his sleep, or had a heart attack brought on by the cancer? I should have stayed longer with him. If I go back to Yichang, I could retrieve the suitcase nuke before it was discovered, and detonate it myself.*

He stopped by the travel agent's booth and changed his ticket to eight in the morning.

If the dam wasn't blown by morning, he would rent a car and drive back, and detonate the bomb. What had happened to Doda?

What if they got Doda to talk? If somehow there was a slip-up. Could someone have betrayed us? Who? There were only four people who knew the plan. Chinese authorities would be looking for me. The first place they would check would be my hotel room. I'm not going to be there. Now he liked the idea of staying in Mei's suite.

Mei opened the door with a relaxed smile. She had changed to a red nightie that almost reached her knees, and she was barefoot. She moved gracefully across the floor; even in the dim light he could see her dark panties and bra through the nightie. His eyes were drawn to her silhouetted lean, muscular body. Her confidence drew him like a magnet.

There were champagne, egg rolls, and dip sauce sitting on the table.

She patted a stuffed chair and he sat down. She poured champagne for both of them, then sat in his lap. "I like to cuddle."

"Where are you from in China?"

"A few miles from the Mongolia border, in the farming area, north of Datong. My mother was Mongolian and my father, Chinese. If you are wondering why I only look part Chinese, it is because my mom has European blood from her ancestors. I looked different from the other girls and used to ask my mother why I looked different. She would say that I looked like her grandmother, who had looked like her grandmother, and that's all she knew. When I was a girl, I would daydream that my rich relatives who lived in Italy would discover their beautiful Chinese granddaughter and come whisk me away to live with them."

"Why Italy?"

"If I was going to have mysterious wealthy relatives, I wanted them to be from someplace warm. When I was a little girl, someone told me that Italy was hot and you could swim in the ocean."

"Did you like living near the Mongolia border?"

"Let me think, it was cold and there was nothing to burn in the fireplace—most of the time. In growing season, we worked from sunrise to sunset to raise the food we ate—I spent a lifetime hungry. Our crops didn't grow well—our diet was rice—usually two meals a day, but in a bad growing season it was one meal a day. The wind was foul half of the year, blowing sand out of Mongolia—into your face and hair. The water from the stream was muddy, and the water from the village well was worse. There was no water to bathe—sometimes there was water in the spring—but there was never any wood to heat the water. How's that? Would you like to move there?"

"It worked for you."

"You mean, wearing a coat made of hand-stitched patches of cloth—on top of each other. I wore it in the day and slept in it at night. Lice lived in the padding and bit you all winter, all spring, and half of the summer. In the warmth of summer, I would take the padded winter clothes and leggings off. I'd wash them in the cold water of the muddy stream. You could see the lice running out of the coat as it got wet, insects that fed off my body. I had lice in my hair all my life. I thought everyone in the world did."

"I take it that you don't want to move back there."

Mei smiled.

"The thing I like about you Rick—is that you catch on quickly."

"I've seen pictures of Manila and it's warm. You can wear sundresses, shorts, bikinis, bathing suits, sunglasses, sun hats, sandals, and the living is easy. No padded clothing with lice, and very few Chinese."

"You know what you want."

"Mei, I may have to take a driving trip tomorrow into China, towards Shanghai. It would help if I could take you; you could serve as my interpreter and help me drive. I will pay you well; could you do that for me?"

Mei took his hand and led Rick into the bedroom.

Rick awoke to a noise coming from the hallway and wondered if they were conducting a search room-by-room for him. He listened intently but heard no more noise and fell back into sleep. Later, when Mei was still asleep, he turned on CNN in the bedroom, but with no sound. It was past one in the morning and still no news. If he had to return to Yichang, then he would take Mei with him. She would be good company and an excellent diversion; no one would pay attention to him. He continued looking at CNN until he dozed off.

He awoke to a late-breaking story. A banner ran across the bottom of the CNN screen. "Industrial explosion at Three Gorges Dam."

He felt relief. Doda had pulled it off. He started getting his clothes on for the eight a.m. flight to Manila. He sat at the table and took out his winnings and counted out half, fifteen thousand dollars. He was scribbling a note to Mei, when she walked out of the bedroom in a short blue nightie and pushed onto half of the chair he was sitting on.

"Don't leave me—I have my passport—I want to go to Manila, with you."

"I have a wife."

"Throw her out."

"It's more complicated than that," Rick said.

"You owe me because I have already set three days aside to accompany you on the trip to Shanghai."

He pushed the fifteen thousand dollars to her side—half of his gambling winnings.

"That's all I get?"

"That's half," Rick said.

"I'm going to move to Manila."

"He pushed another five thousand over."

"I want your card. Will you sponsor me?" Mei said.

"Yes."

He slid his business card over with the cash.

"I like being kind to you." Her arms slid to encircle his neck and she rested her face against his.

"Do you have to go?"

Rick boarded the Philippines Airline jet with his eyes glued to the still-breaking story of the Three Gorges Dam; the story was still developing. *He wondered when the dam had been destroyed.*

Mei discreetly followed Rick to the airport. In her jogging suit and sunglasses, she mingled with the crowd, tactfully watching Rick until he boarded the Air Philippines flight to Manila. When the plane had departed, Mei sent a text message to a company owned by Zang Tao: "My friends are gone."

Chapter 9

A WALL OF water—almost four hundred feet in height, more than a mile across, beyond two hundred miles long—swept past the dams; vaporized the retaining wall. The dam's structure was completely gone. The initial blast had created an enormous vapor cloud—the explosion pushed the water in the upper Yangtze back—but now it sped past with the fury of a tsunami.

The escaping wall of water began draining the upper Yangtze. The sudden swirling current left hundreds of boats of all sizes beached, lying on their side, capsized or broken into pieces as they were swept along by the escaping water of the Yangtze seeking its new level. The only vessels having a chance of surviving this malicious current were more than fifty miles upstream, but after fifteen minutes the current was too fast, too strong, and too swirling; it was unnavigable.

In the Yangtze, below Yichang, there was an incalculable amount of damage. The water trapped in the reservoir poured through the vaporized dam unhindered. Four hundred feet high—more than a mile wide—moving with breathtaking speed, it slammed into everything in its path exploding houses, boats, and bridges. The debris caught up in the fast-moving water was as deadly as the drowning water of the Yangtze. Still the Yangtze raced towards the East China Sea flooding houses, factories and farms as it sought its new level.

Finally, the Yangtze began losing its momentum, more than ten hours later. It flooded low-lying deltas, and swept across Shanghai, and poured into the East China Sea. As the birds flew along the river, there was devastation from Chongqing to Shanghai—more than three hundred miles of destruction.

The source of electrical power for central China was gone. The source of cheap transportation for central China, the Yangtze, was again unnavigable by large vessels. Agriculture would again be at the peril of the flooding tides of the Yangtze River. The loss of life was in the thousands; the damage was enormous; and the economic damage was incalculable. If China was a giant, this blow had staggered the giant and brought it to one knee.

All day, the major world networks carried the story. A few news channels reported nothing else. It was difficult to get any Chinese officials to comment; they were all tight-lipped, everyone waiting for an official press release from Beijing. Later in the day the news channels were being restricted access to the site. They continued repeating the same scenes: photos of massive flooding downstream of the dam, and bodies and debris floating in the water.

Initially, the theory had been that the one of the dam's thirty giant generators had exploded. This explosion caused other generators to short circuit, and it quickly expanded to all thirty generators. The domino effect resulted in a massive explosion.

Engineering consultants hired by the major news organizations were saying that in order for the Three Gorges Dam, with all its cement and steel construction, to vanish as it did, the cause could only be extreme heat. The temperature range required to make something as massive as the Three Gorges Dam vaporize could only have come from a nuclear source.

The news stations were now showing military helicopters deploying soldiers, wearing blue contamination suits, setting up checkpoints, miles from the dam.

A restricted area was being set up six miles to the east and west of the dam. But forward of the dam, the controlled area extended more than thirty miles. It appeared that everything was contaminated.

Chapter 10

Beijing, China

CHANG WEI WAS the chief investigator for Wang Xiu Ying, who was head of state security and a member of the Politburo Assembly. Chang Wei stood before Wang Xiu Ying, who sat at his desk and stared.

"Chang, what do we know for sure, that is verifiable with facts?"

"We know for a fact that it was a nuclear device, because of the amount of radiation produced. Also, the high temperatures caused the cement and steel beams to vaporize, and the extensive damage was created by one explosion," Chang said.

"And?" Wang raised his hands from the desk.

"We know, from aircraft photo images, that the blast occurred near the center of the dam and below the surface, and probably close to the bottom of the dam's retaining wall. The hole was largest there and for this reason took the brunt of the initial explosion. The vast amount of vapor reported was because the energy heat of the bomb vaporized millions of cubic feet of water. This created an enormous quantity of vapor that hung in the air, which slowly drifted to the ground, and the vapor contaminated everything it touched."

"Do you have a radiation signature?" Wang said.

"Yes, it's been verified three times and from three different areas of contamination. This proves there was just one nuclear detonation, and that the radiation signature of the fuel used for the nuclear device was U-235."

"Where did the bomb come from?" Wang said.

Wang was now standing and pacing the room, rubbing his hands together.

"It was not a Chinese nuclear weapon radiation signature. For this reason, we believe the bomb was brought into China from outside."

"How did this nuclear bomb get into China?" Wang said.

Wang was rubbing his face with both hands, as if he had just been awakened by bad news. He continued pacing the floor.

"Sir, that has not been determined as of this date. However, we have an enormous investigation in process." Chang said.

"This investigation is not moving along fast enough."

"Sir, the People's security police recordings are records of all communications and were kept seventeen miles away at district police headquarters. The records survived the explosion. They indicated that a patrol boat responded to a proximity sensor that turned on security lighting at the retaining wall on the high side of the dam. All the videotape and cameras were destroyed in the blast, but we are still searching."

"I need more, much more. How did this nuclear device get on Chinese territory? That is a critical question." Wang said.

Wang continued to pace and rub his hands together.

"Chang, sit down! I want you to write down these questions. Why did they sabotage the Three Gorges Dam? Why not a military target? Why not the center of Beijing? Why not the financial center of Shanghai? Why not one of our major airports? Why not the vast ocean port in Shanghai? Why not The Peoples Party Communist Party Headquarters?"

Wang paused.

"I know you have all your investigators on this, but I want you to pull people from other departments; anyone you need. You must have investigators searching everywhere; go through everything. You must question everyone, and I don't care who they are. You have my authority to detained or arrest anyone. You are to spare no expense. Go anywhere and do anything you need to do, but find something.

"Chang, I want facts, be absolutely sure of what you report."

"Sir, the biggest difficulty we face is that the bomb destroyed the evidence that could have been used to trace what happened and when it happened. The radiation has contaminated the entire site of the explosion. All reports and records from the tourist boat offices and pedestrian sign-in logs were vaporized in the initial blast. Happy Village was destroyed in the explosion. There is nothing remaining. All the video cameras and video recordings were melted or vaporized during the first explosion."

"I understand it is difficult. But somewhere there is evidence. Get the new police cadets training class—that's more than three-hundred cadets—put them in contamination suits and use them to search the containment areas for evidence." Wang said.

Chang quit writing and dropped his pen on the desk.

"Sir, are you sure? It will cause their death or severe radiation poisoning!"

"Yes, I understand. I do not want to lose experienced officers. Use cadets. Find evidence now!"

Chapter 11

WHEN HE WAS thirteen years of age Zang Tao hauled industrial garments from the clothing factories to the train station with his large handcart—he was the mule. He would wait at the train station for the rolls of cloth to arrive, load them on the cart, and pull and push the fabric rolls to the factories.

It was a meager living, pulling a handcart. It was the business his father started; it sparsely fed his family. His father worked long hours every day until his death of a heart ailment at the age of twenty-nine. Now, Zang Tao was harnessed to the inherited pull cart. The thing he liked least about the job was that you used so much energy pulling the heavy cart. He was always hungry, and his earnings were so meager he couldn't afford to properly feed himself.

He provided for his gloomy, broken-hearted mother, a younger sister with a disabled leg from birth, and a brother born after his father's death. He got jobs for his pull cart because he bid the lowest price and paid the factory manager a kickback.

While waiting for a cloth shipment to arrive, he ran across an ancient sewing machine that was damaged and abandoned in the baggage area of the train station.

He made a deal to empty the train toilets and clean the bathrooms five times a day, from early in the morning until almost midnight, as the train stopped five time a day, for three months, in exchange for the sewing machine. He emptied the toilets and cleaned the bathrooms for another three months, to get the money to purchase the parts needed to repair the sewing machine and pay the village mechanic to help him.

Later, he purchased throw-away garments and poorly-dyed cloth from the factories he hauled supplies to, and kicked money back to the shop managers. On his daily cart hauls, he stopped to see everyone, and found his garments easy to sell because he was the cheapest.

Zang Tao was barely making a profit. He knew if he could increase his volume, then he would make a reasonable profit. He soon realized his fingers weren't fast enough, or nimble enough. The nights were too short, and he didn't have enough time.

He loaded the ancient sewing machine on his handcart. He made a deal with a widow and her daughters: they would sew the garments he told them to produce. He would provide the cloth and pay them for each garment sewn. They started in the center of the largest room in their three-room hut.

Zang Tao concentrated on buying the cloth, selling the garments in volume, and paying the kickbacks. He was already a member of the People's Communist Youth. He became more active; he wanted the connections and support. He always made it a point to stay in the good graces of the local communist officials, and he always contributed generously.

Zang Tao found his strengths were as a deal-maker, hiring people to manage the shops, opening more sewing shops, and dealing with people. He had a ready smile, a pleasing nature, and an inborn instinct about people, and he liked helping people. He enjoyed making money and understood the benefits of spreading the wealth.

He developed loyal managers and encouraged purchasing agents to steer business his way. The supportive communist officials who liked his money used their authority to protect Zang Tao and his growing empire. His customers purchased his products because his prices were the cheapest and he didn't cheat them. The few disputes that arose from older, more experienced businessmen who tried to take advantage of his youth were resolved in his favor, thanks to his friends in the local communist party.

When China's economy opened up for entrepreneurship, he was a natural. Then Zang Tao had access to loans from government banks and took care of the local officials. He knew how to work with China's bureaucracy.

He was a hard worker and a gifted deal-maker and found the capitalist system easy to understand cheap prices. He quickly made connections through Hong Kong to foreign markets. Soon his small shops were becoming factories, then turning into large, very busy companies. He pushed low prices and aggressively sought more business, and later he concentrated on improving product quality.

Inside twenty years, he had more than a thousand factories of all sizes that made products from shirts to electronics. He was a talented manager of people and knew how to inspire them, and his employees were excited about working for him; he treated them fairly and never cheated them.

As his business empire grew, so did his girth. He weighed almost four hundred pounds. Soon Zang Tao was renowned throughout Asia; no one forgot his name or his appearance. Zang Tao was a large man, with enormous wealth, and his appearance didn't embarrass him.

He remembered his exhaustion from pushing and pulling the hauling cart—always starved, scrambling for rice, spoiled vegetables, and scraps of fish—a luxury for him and his father's family; a family he struggled every day to feed; family that he promised his father to care for until his death. Now prosperous, he liked to eat well and often; he made no apologies for his weight.

The standing joke in China's business community was "Who is China's largest private employer?" Of course, they would all say—"Zang Tao, The Whale"—and laugh so hard they had to hold their sides.

In later years, when the Politburo opened up a portion of their membership to successful business owners, Zang Tao was their first choice. He had brought considerable prosperity to China through his factories, and he treated his employees well. He was viewed by the Politburo as knowing how to do business in capitalist countries, and as being a very effective and extremely efficient manager. All the party officials he dealt with liked him; he had paid them well.

Zang Tao saw in the Politburo an excellent opportunity for new connections and additional prosperity. He was not really political, but believed in China, and its work ethic.

Zang Tao's greatest regret was that he missed his exciting gambling trips to Las Vegas. In Vegas, Zang Tao was called "The Whale" not because of his bulk, but because of his great wealth. He threw tens of millions of dollars around lavishly and foolishly, and he didn't care because he was far away—from the prying eyes of China.

He cherished the drink with the bubbles that made his throat tingle. Most of all, he loved the three beautiful, pale-skinned women, their skin so translucent he could see their blue veins. Their exotic long golden hair brushed against his skin and they treated him so gently—he relaxed.

Slowly his mind would drift away and—go on vacation. He shuddered as he remembered their golden hair touching his skin; how his skin tingled. He liked touching the golden strands with his fingers; it was soft and fluffy, as light as the air. Their soft hands on his skin, as they bathed him, and those warm hands slowly massaging fragrant oil into his skin. Their angelic laughter in that strange language, their soft voices as they hummed songs that filled the bathhouse with a rhythm that stirred something inside him. They called him Buddha; in Vegas he felt like a god. Las Vegas was such a delicious decadence.

He had been a member of the Politburo for five years and was viewed as a rising star. At today's inquiry concerning the destruction of the Three Gorges Dam, the Politburo Standing Committee had asked Zang Tao to conduct the questioning.

Wang Xiu Ying stood before the Politburo Standing Committee and could feel all eyes on him. Prime Minister Li Wei looked at Zang Tao and nodded his head.

"Speak to us, Wang Xiu Ying," Zang Tao said.

"My report will initially deal with information that has been verified.

"First, the explosion was caused by a nuclear detonation. This is proven by the extent of damage caused by a single explosion. Secondly, there are vast amounts of radiation. Third, we have used some of the radiation samples to establish the signature of the bomb. Fourth, the fuel that initiated the explosion was U-235. And last, the signature indicates it was not a Chinese nuclear device—it's of foreign manufacture."

"What is going to be your line of investigation? How are you going to proceed?" Zang Tao said. He put his large hands under his triple chin and stared at Wang.

"I'm proceeding as follows: we are currently combing thru the nuclear blast site looking for any evidence. This is complicated by the enormous amount of areas that are underwater. This is very dangerous because of the instability of the area, and also high levels of radiation. Additionally, we are pursuing how the nuclear device entered into China."

"How are you doing that?" Zang Tao said. He placed his hands back under his chin.

"We are currently pulling all computer images of material shipped into China and carefully reviewing these images again. We are looking for a hidden nuclear device. Additionally, we have requested that all of our agents posted abroad be reassigned to investigate any leads concerning this affair."

"Are there more nuclear devices that are hidden in China that are going to be detonated?" Zang Tao said.

Wang was caught off guard. He was not used to being talked to like this. He took a moment to gather his thoughts.

"State security is excellent at all of our ocean ports and borders. Internal security is of the highest caliber. We monitor what is being moved anywhere in China. Our paper trails are detailed and allow us to trace any shipment to and from anywhere. We have the best internal security in the world."

Zang Tao stared at Wang. His face was solemn.

"Wang Xiu Ying, you are in charge of state security. You have failed to answer my question. Are there any more nuclear devices in China waiting to be detonated?" Zang Tao said.

Wang's facial expression was snarled, and he looked in disgust at the obese Zang Tao, but held his tongue.

"There are no nuclear devices waiting to be detonated in China," Wang said.

"How did the nuclear device get into China?" Zang Tao said.

"I'm not sure," Wang said.

"Then there has been a breach in state security."

"Probably."

"Not probably. State security has been breached," Zang Tao said.

"Yes, that appears to be the answer."

"Then you don't know if there are more nuclear devices on Chinese territory, in other places, waiting to be detonated."

"I feel very strongly that there aren't more nuclear devices on Chinese territory," Wang said.

"I don't share your feelings. One nuclear device has detonated. We don't know how it got on Chinese territory. We don't know if there are more already in place, hidden and waiting to be detonated. We don't know who did this, we don't even know why," Zang Tao said.

Zang Tao paused. He looked at Wang, who was standing in front of his chair and leaning forward with both hands on the table and a sneer on his face.

"Are you capable of solving this mystery?" Zang Tao said.

Wang had taken off his glasses and was wiping them with a tissue.

"Do you need help leading this investigation?" Zang Tao said.

Wang, his face twisted with anger, his nostrils flaring and his body rigid, slowly composed himself and placed his glasses back on his face, then addressed the question.

"I'm fully capable of resolving this problem, and it will get resolved; it is truly just a matter of time. We have a massive investigation in progress; nothing will escape our scrutiny."

Zang Tao and Wang stared at each other.

"You don't understand. We don't have time. We don't know how your security was breached and we don't know if there are other nuclear devices waiting to be detonated."

Zang Tao turned his face to the other committee members.

"I think it is necessary that we appoint someone to work with Wang Xiu Ying, and that person must report directly to this committee."

"That is not necessary," Wang said.

The committee members glared harshly at Wang Xiu Ying.

Chapter 12

Beijing, China

TWENTY-TWO DAYS later an unofficial report circulated that the Three Gorges Dam had been an act of terrorism. It was a nuclear detonation and not of Chinese manufacture. Additionally, the Peoples Liberation Army had no nuclear devices of any type in the Three Gorges Area. There was to be an official announcement by the spokesperson for the Politburo, to be followed by a national statement from Chinese Prime Minister Li Wei.

A CNN nightly news anchor summed up the Chinese development.

"Chinese officials have learned that the Nuclear Device, which they are calling a compact nuclear bomb, was shipped to the port of Shanghai. It was hidden in a large shipment of industrial machinery and was transported on a commercial vessel bearing the flag of the Philippines. It has been further learned that the cargo had been loaded onto this ship from fourteen different ports.

"All shipments entering Chinese ports have to be computer imaged; those images are stored in computer archives. It's the port's computer files that allowed us to solve how, when, and where this compact nuclear bomb arrived on Chinese soil."

Next, the Chinese Prime Minister Li Wei spoke from behind a podium. His face was solemn and as he began to speak his voice was harsh.

"As you have just learned, a compact nuclear bomb was deliberately concealed and illegally shipped to China. Although the People's Port Authorities have adequate safeguards to prevent this from happening, six Shanghai port officials accepted bribes and turned their backs on their responsibilities and duty to China."

He stopped talking, as a video screen showed the images of six men. They were standing one behind the other. Their hands were handcuffed behind their backs. Each was being led by a uniformed policeman who had one hand on their arm. A thick hangman's noose was already around their necks and hung about a foot down their backs, it had a hook in the end. The short rope would be hooked to the gallows rope. The expressions on their faces were grim and resigned to their fate. They were on the way to the gallows to be hung, and their execution would be carried out within minutes. It was a disturbing video, and designed to send a message.

Again Li Wei spoke.

"Because we have kept all images of material shipped to the Port of Shanghai, we were able to trace where and how this compact nuclear bomb entered our country. We are now in the process of tracking down where the small nuclear device originated and who manufactured it. We have determined the Asian source of some of the parts and we are deeply troubled by this. I will report more about this when this investigation is finished.

"The Politburo Standing Committee no longer believes that the terrorist act of the Three Gorges Dam was to open the waterway to allow a greater flow of water to our neighbor to the south. It was a deliberate act to sabotage the Chinese economy by eliminating the electrical output from the Three Gorges Dam, which provides fifteen percent of the total energy supplied to the Chinese national electrical grid. It's this electrical network that has helped our manufacturing industry, and the People's Republic of China, to flourish.

"This deliberate act of sabotage has caused losses in excess of fifty trillion yuan to the Chinese economy currently, and will continue to accumulate losses for some years into the future. We will hunt down the evil people who have attacked our beloved nation. China will recover every yuan that has been robbed from the Chinese people."

Manila, Philippines

General Mendoza watched the CNN News and thought, *Looks like the Chinese have chosen someone to put the blame on. They have probably identified the timing device we installed.*

Chapter 13

Tokyo, Japan

JAPANESE PRIME MINISTER Okada Taka sat in his office, staring at Chinese Prime Minister Li Wei addressing the Chinese people. The large TV screen was translating his Chinese words into Japanese as quickly as they left his mouth. The phrase, "Asian source of some of the parts and we are deeply troubled by this" did not bode well for Japan, Prime Minister Okada thought.

He knew Li Wei hated the Japanese. He hailed from Nanjing; all Chinese peasants had it ingrained into their heads that Japanese soldiers had raped all the women of Nanjing. They called it the 'Rape of Nanjing' and Li Wei was a peasant and would always be a peasant in his mind.

In truth, most of the infantry soldiers of the Japanese Central China Command were volunteers and forced recruits from Korea. They were brutal due to their peasant life of hardship. They were grateful to trade their rags for Japanese army uniforms. They received three handfuls of rice and half a fish a day; a few yen each month; all they could pilfer from the Chinese villages they swept through; and fire to sleep by. Of course, the 'Sauce of the Rice' for joining the Japanese army was to take revenge on their Chinese neighbor who had heaped centuries of abuse on the Korean people.

He smiled to himself; perhaps Chinese Prime Minister Li Wei was part Korean. He found this amusing. General Matsui was hung for the Rape of Nanjing, a scapegoat. The Chinese had done worse. And the Americans, they dropped atomic bombs on entire city populations that weren't even justified military targets. Incinerating and vaporizing thousands, all that remained of some poor souls was their silhouettes burned into cement. At least Pearl Harbor was a military target. History has always honored the winner over the vanquished. *The lesson taught by history—don't lose a war.*

He looked back at the big screen. The Chinese Prime Minster was turning away from the podium, his face as grim as when he started his national address. Prime Minister Okada turned and looked at his informal cabinet, seven men whom he could trust. They weren't all members of his political party, but they were astute advisors.

"I don't think the peasant Li Wei owns a smile," Okada said.

There was laughter in the room and it helped to break the tension. He stood up and began pacing, then leaned against the wall.

"Is there anyone here who thinks that Li Wei will not blame the destruction of the Three Gorges Dam on Japan?"

Seven men sat looking at him.

"Does he have a choice?" Saito Hiroki, a Naval commander, said.

"He could tell the truth," Fujii Naoki said.

"What is the truth?" Saito Hiroki said.

Then all eyes shifted to Okada, still leaning against the wall. He lifted his hands, palms up, in frustration.

"I don't know who did what. I can say unequivocally that we had no involvement; it was not us; it was not Japan."

He paused.

"Personally I think it is some type of internal strife. A frustrated group, ethnic, religious, perhaps even peasants who were forced from their land to make way for the vast water reservoir the dam required."

"We have leaked information that the Chinese investigators have some type of proof that Japanese timing and ignition systems were found to be part of the nuclear device," Okada said.

"No way. Every part of the bomb would be vaporized." Sato Kento, the National Defense Adviser, said.

"They have something they're going to use to point the finger at us," Okada said.

"Why? Why Japan? WWII is a long time gone," Meno said.

"I agree. They hate us, but there's got to be more to this. We have hundreds of factories in China that employ tens of thousands of people." Zeno, minister of finance, said.

"Maybe they don't know who did it, but are going to use this as an excuse to seek reparations they feel are justified from WWII," Sato said.

"Perhaps a reason to take some of our islands, and push for dominance of the East China Sea, and South China Sea. If we resist with conventional military forces, then they will strike with tactical nuclear weapons; which we don't have." Okada said.

Now several heads were nodding.

"Japan didn't nuke their precious Three Gorges Dam, but they certainly could use it as a pretext to attack Japan, and seek control over the East China Sea," Fujii said.

"If they can create enough confusion in Washington to make them believe that Japan did indeed have something to do with the Three Gorges disaster, that could be a serious problem. Actually, they don't have to convince Washington, just the American News organizations. Without public support, it will freeze the hands of the politicians, which will prevent the American military from honoring their nuclear umbrella commitments to Japan." Ishii, a professor of history at Tokyo University, said.

"I think what you're saying is true, if they don't attack our mainland where the American military bases are. But the outlying islands—America won't support the treaty. We lose a few islands and the Chinese gain control over the East China Sea, its oil and gas deposits. They also impede our commercial shipping lanes and obtain a distinct military advantage," Okada said.

He stood looking at all their faces.

"Is this what Prime Minister Li Wei, and the Politburo Standing Committee are up to?" Okada said.

There were five out of seven heads nodding yes.

"We have a consensus. But I didn't say yes. Because I don't know what the Politburo is thinking. They are not fundamentally of the same mind as the Prime Minister Li, or even the Standing Committee. The Politburo members are traditionalists and, as a rule, are cautious. If Li Wei pulls this feat off, they will have to back him; he will be too powerful," Ishii said, as the informal cabinet members filed out of the office.

Chapter 14

OKADA SAID, "SATO, please stay for a few minutes."

"Are all preparations completed for operation renegade?"

"All activities are complete; everything is planned out to the smallest detail," Sato said.

"Yes, that's good. I don't want to, but we may have to implement operation renegade soon."

"We're ready."

"Have you considered what could go wrong?" Okada said.

"Yes, in operational planning we have taken each critical procedure and caused it to fail. Then we have strategically planned around that failed process. We have successfully fulfilled the mission every time." Sato said.

"Where is the greatest risk?" Okada said.

"The risk that is the greatest is overpowering the crew on the American nuclear submarine. There we must rely on deception. Eddie Yoshida is the Japanese-American, who attended the Naval Academy, and spent twenty-three years in the American Navy, and more than fifteen years in their submarine service. He commanded an American nuclear sub for his last six years. He was the engineering officer for the Hercules on its maiden voyage. Later he was its commander for almost three years."

"This is the man who married your wife's youngest sister?"

"Yes. I approached him—he did not approach us. Eddie did not agree to it at first, but thought about for it for about three months. As relations with China deteriorated, we discussed the situation in Asia, at family events and in my home, many times before he agreed to do it. I recruited him. I trust him with my life," Sato said.

"What about his life before coming to Japan?"

"His wife died of cancer, about four years before he retired from the Navy. They had no children. He moved to Tokyo and met Kaori, at the Buddha Temple; that's my wife's youngest sister. They have been married for eight years and have two children. He is a good man and a loyal friend. He can be trusted, and we need him."

"Eddie has been training our crew for the last year on how to man each critical station on the submarine Hercules. I'm impressed with his exhaustive knowledge of every duty station. We cannot do this operation without him."

Okada nodded his head for Sato to continue.

"Eddie now lives in Tokyo and his allegiance is with Japan. He does not believe that America will honor its commitment to Japan, under the nuclear umbrella agreement."

"This Japanese-American Naval Academy Officer, who spent his entire career in the American Navy—will he betray America?" Okada said.

"Eddie doesn't see it as a betrayal of America. He feels it is the best way to prevent a nuclear exchange between China and America. He believes that China will gamble that American will not honor its commitment, and eventually will attack Japan."

"How does this Eddie feel about Japan having its own nuclear arsenal?" Okada said.

"Eddie feels this is the best solution. If Japan has its own nuclear arsenal, then China will not attack. China will know that

Japan doesn't have to depend on the Americans. Japan will defend it islands, its shipping lanes, and its sovereignty."

"It would be expedient if I could meet this Japanese-American myself and get a feel for him. Of course, the risk is far too great because I must be able to deny I know him." Okada said.

"Prime Minister, Eddie has married into my family. He is my brother-in-law, both his parents were Japanese, and he has lived in Japan for eight years. I had our security services do an exhaustive background check on Eddie more than two years ago. Eddie is who he purports to be."

"What else?"

"Eddie Yoshida is the key to taking the American nuclear submarine. It's his experience that we are counting on to deceive the crew for at least ten minutes. Once we are in position on the submarine and undetected, we will take the sub, and when we exit the harbor, the greatest risk will be over. Once we get the sub into the open sea, we will disappear without a trace."

"How long before the nuclear missiles are operational and under Japanese control?"

"We have our technicians prepped and standing by with all necessary equipment. We will have to remove American navigation devices, safety checks, and communications systems. Then we will place the warheads on our own missiles. We will need twenty-four hours and we will at least have some of the missiles operational; then it's a matter of getting them deployed. Once in position, Japan will have a submersible nuclear missile deterrent ready to defend Japan."

"I know this hasn't been easy. You have done an excellent job, and this won't be forgotten."

"Thank you, Prime Minister Okada Taka."

Chapter 15

Okinawa, Japan

FROM ASIA'S MAINLAND, clouds from the monsoon season drifted out to sea dropping moisture in the South China Sea, and beyond. On Okinawa, dark clouds obscured the moon and rain pounded the island, reducing visibility to less than to fifty feet.

Eddie Yoshida sat in the SUV observing the US nuclear submarine Hercules from a discreet distance. A submarine, when in port, is in its most defenseless position. He also knew that naval submarine regulations required a nuclear submarine, when not at its home port, to be able to put to sea within fifteen minutes. For the nuclear-powered Hercules to do that required a crew of at least thirty-four sailors and officers. He was also confident that the senior officers and crew members would be ashore after spending at least two months under the water. Only a few junior grade officers and a skeleton crew would remain on board, just enough to comply with naval regulations.

In the darkness, four trucks without lights approached a back gate at the American Naval Base. The Okinawan security guard quickly opened the gate and waved them through. The camera lens was temporarily covered. No entry was noted in the log and no authorization was requested.

The four trucks parked in a darkened area where the security lighting had been temporarily disconnected for repair. The eight men in the SUV waited for the trucks to get into position. They slowly moved forward another hundred yards before turning on the headlights, and continuing forward towards the American nuclear submarine Hercules.

The seaman deck sentinel dressed in rain gear stood leaning against the tower wall and was half asleep. When he opened his eyes, he saw three petty officers and five high-ranking naval officers; one appeared to be an admiral, and they were already walking up the gangplank. A little muddled, he did not activate the intercom, but instead snapped to attention and saluted.

Eddie Yoshida, dressed in US Naval Rear Admiral's uniform, returned the seaman's salute. "What is your name sailor?"

"Seaman Baxter, sir."

"Sailor, this is a readiness inspection by the office of the inspecting admiral; you are to stand down. Our credentials have already been verified at the main gate. Seamen Towel will man your post with you. Do you read me, Seaman Baxter?" Admiral Yoshida said.

"Yes, sir."

"Then stand down."

Admiral Yoshida turned to his adjutant.

"Begin recording the official transcript of the Readiness Inspection Test. Key in the time and date and start the recording. We are now boarding the Hercules and conducting our readiness inspection." He climbed down the ladder from the wing, followed by four other officers. The submarine's office of the day, Ensign Crowly, was surprised, but snapped to attention, and saluted the Admiral.

"Ensign Crowly, I'm Admiral Yoshida and we're conducting a readiness test for the office of the inspecting admiral." As he was speaking, the four officers accompanying him climbed down the wing and started fanning out inside the sub. The officer who reached the environmental controls room immediately opened and stuck a container of invisible and odorless sirus gas into the ventilation system. The officer entering the rear compartment opened a container and it drifted into the ship's central passageway. In all, four officers opened sirus gas canisters, and within sixty seconds, the entire ship was filled with sirus gas. As Admiral Yoshida was talking with Ensign Crowly, he watched the Ensign stagger, then caught him as he collapsed and laid him on the on the deck.

Admiral Yoshida and his crew had already been inoculated so that the sirus gas would not affect them. They had three hours to give an anti-sirus inoculation to the unconscious American sailors, or they would die from sirus gas poisoning.

One of the officers accompanying Admiral Yoshida ascended the ladder and looked at Seaman Baxter, who lay dead on the deck with a slit throat. He raised his hand above his head and waved. Fifty-three men hiding in the dark quickly made their way to the submarine Hercules. The men assigned to the mooring crew began disconnecting the ship from its moorings and shore electrical power and water lines. The men entering the sub stepped over the unconscious American bodies, as they quickly moved to their stations. Admiral Yoshida spoke, "Eight minutes and we must be underway." The men immediately started executing their tasks at their assigned duty stations, having been drilled by Eddie Yoshida repeatedly for more than a year.

Admiral Yoshida took charge of the control center as the Hercules began to edge away from its moorings. He depressed the red button on a Japanese handset, transmitting the signal the

Hercules was underway and to open the control gates. He wanted to be past the control gates in seven minutes.

Outside the naval sea gate control tower, three men dressed in black unleashed Sirus gas into the ventilation system, waited three minutes, then entered the tower. The officer, petty officer, and seaman manning the control gates were unconscious. They quickly took control of the sea entrance and exit gates. They waited for a signal from the Hercules before they would begin opening the gates.

A diode on his high-frequency handset lit red.

"They're moving, let's get the gates open."

Eddie saw the green diode light up on his handset, indicating the gate control tower had been secured.

The sub, moving slowly, turned its nose towards the control gates, then moved steadily forward. He watched on the remote screen as the infrared cameras brought the control gate into view. On the side screen, he saw the control tower up close as they passed. Now switching to the rear screen, he saw the control tower fading away. In seven minutes time, the Hercules had passed through the control gates and into the open sea.

The men clad in black stood in the shadows of the control tower and watched as the noiseless black sub passed like a giant shadow through the gates. They quickly closed the gates, placed the controls in the locked position, and slipped into the night.

Four trucks and an SUV passed back through the rear gate. A sign was placed on the gate that read 'temporarily closed' and the gate was locked. The camera was lens uncovered. The Japanese paramilitary man disguised as a security guard climbed aboard the last truck. In the weeds nearby lay a dead Okinawa gate guard.

"Secure to dive. Dive to one hundred fifty feet. Heading twelve degrees, make way at sixteen knots. We are preparing to rendezvous with the freighter in six nautical miles." Eddie said.

Eddie thought, *we have escaped undetected so far, and this was the most critical stage. Now we're in the open sea and I can run and hide. The freighter will be moving slow at ten knots. I will approach from the rear and slide under that noisy beast, and hide the Hercules's reactor signature in all that mechanical noise.*

He watched the freighter on the radar screen tracking nine knots. At two miles north of the freighter, he ordered to periscope depth. He saw the ship with all of its lights. It looked like a Christmas tree floating on the water.

A single flash of their signal light indicated they were ready to receive the submarine. It was prearranged that all signals would be visual and one way only. This way there would be no communication trail to follow.

He waited until the freighter passed in front of them.

"Capitan Hokoa, bring her left twenty-seven degrees."

This brought them a quarter mile directly behind the freighter. With all of its lights displayed it was an easy target to slide under.

"Capital Hokoa, increase speed to fourteen knots."

"Captain Hokoa, we're under the freighter. Bring our depth to eighty feet. Match her speed of nine knots and stay with her course."

"This is the noisiest freighter ever, Admiral Yoshida," the radioman said.

"That's because there are three electronic noise generators helping out."

"Let me know if there is a sudden burst of communications from the American naval base and make a note of the time," Eddie said.

Eddie wondered if the Hercules had been reported missing. The Japanese air force was monitoring the American military communications networks. He would know soon enough, but the longer, the better.

East China Sea

Eddie left the attack and command center. Working his way from duty station to duty station, checking the controls, going over the procedures for each duty station. He spent a lot of time going over the procedures for turning down the reactor with Lieutenant Ito. It was approaching six in the morning and the cargo ship had traveled almost thirty-eight nautical miles.

Eddie moved back to the command center but stumbled over Ensign Crowly's extended foot. He landed on one knee and his outstretched hand. His face only a few inches away from Ensign Crowly's face, he heard his breathing. It was so shallow his chest barely moved. He got up quickly and walked to the navigation console.

Eddie waited as the massive cargo ship veered to within two miles of the small island of Miso, its customary route for over a year.

"Lt. Ito, shut down the reactor; we will now operate on reserve battery power.

"Captain Hokoa, increase your depth to one-hundred-twenty-five feet and left 14 degrees towards the east end of the island.

"In one nautical mile bring us to a dead stop."

Eddie was scanning the remote screens looking for the colored lights that marked the entrance to the cave. The Hercules slowed to a creep, as it moved to within a quarter-mile of the stone cliffs.

"Captain Hokan, proceed at a snail's pace; we do not want to run into a rock formation.

"Captain Hokan, I have a visual on the remote camera screen; these color coded lights are the approach lane to the cavern. Keep the red to the starboard side."

Eddie heard tapping on the sail hatch as divers began preparations to assist in easing the Hercules into the mammoth cavern. Two large mechanical arms, one on each side of the hull, helped position the still-floating submarine to a cushioned, V-shaped resting berth.

The berth was six hundred feet long, more than was necessary to accommodate the five hundred sixty foot long and eighteen thousand ton nuclear submarine. Then the enormous door slowly slid shut.

The cavern ceiling had been removed all the way to the surface. A huge hanger served as its top cover. An airplane passing over would only see a large industrial storage building. But underneath was an enormous cavern, and when the water was pumped out it became a clandestine underground dry dock. Seventeen massive industrial and muffled pumps elevated the water from the cavern to the surface and into a river that flowed out to sea. Some of the pumps continued to slowly operate, as seawater tended to seep through the reinforced walls and around the seals on the massive door. This secretive cavern had been constructed over a five-year period as a shelter and dry dock for Japanese home defense force submarines, and as a place for refuge, for reloading, and a dry dock for repairs, in the event of hostilities. Now it would serve as a temporary shelter for the Hercules.

Eddie Yoshida watched the remote camera screen and could hear water being pumped out. In less than an hour, the cavern lit up. A few minutes later, he heard a tapping on the sail hatch. He ordered the hatch opened. Light flooded into the sub, illuminating the control and attack center. Eddie Yoshida climbed out of the hatch. It was like daylight inside the cavern. High above a massive amount of industrial lights were attached to the metal grid. The grid was lowered to just seventy feet above the Hercules; already he could feel the heat from the lamps. There were still large, shallow puddles of seawater scattered across the cavern floor, and he could see fish splashing as they tried to survive in unaccustomed shallow water.

Eddie Yoshida looked at his watch.

"Captain Hokan, it's seven a.m. on Okinawa; if they haven't discovered the Hercules is missing, they will shortly."

Chapter 16

American Naval Base
Okinawa

AS THE DAWN broke, and sunlight began poking through holes in the water-laden clouds, the USS naval tender ship Hillsdale tried to enter the naval dock area, but couldn't raise anyone in the gate control tower. They waited more than an hour. Finally pissed off, the radioman was able to rouse Seaman Rogers in the repair parts depot to answer the phone. Half asleep, Seaman Rogers said he would walk over and wake them up, but first he drank a cup of Jo.

Seaman Rogers slowly ambled through humid ocean air to wake up the gate crew who had obviously fallen asleep. This wasn't unusual; he had made this early morning stroll several times before. This time when be banged open the door to scare the shit out of everyone, no one jumped out of their seat or lifted their sleepy head off of a desk. No one stirred. He pushed Seaman Thompson on the shoulder and his friend fell out of his seat—dead on the floor.

The Hercules wasn't missed until Lieutenant Banning entered the dock area at 7:34 in the morning, after a night of heavy drinking. He had made a pass at everything in a skirt. He remembered that, but couldn't remember going to bed, but that's where he woke up, and with a giant headache. Another night lost to booze; fifty-eight days of underwater sub patrol will do that to you.

He stood there looking at the dock where the submarine Hercules should be. He turned and walked a half-mile across the dock area to the east mooring area. He saw one diesel sub. Feeling disorientated and a little embarrassed, he starting walking towards the gate control tower to check on the sub's berthing location.

It was less than a half-hour since the bodies were discovered. The base operations officer had just walked in the door and was staring at the dead sailors. Now the base commander was arriving. He had been drinking with the brass of the Hercules last night and looked horrible, and felt worse.

Upon entering, he looked at the bodies and told the operations office to place the entire base on priority-one alert.

The operations officer picked up the phone and the base sirens began wailing the alarm. The base commander looked at the gate controls. They were in locked position. Three men were dead, but it was unclear what had caused their death.

As Lieutenant Banning entered, the base commander remembered him from last night's drinking session.

"What do you want?"

"I can't find where the Hercules is berthed."

"West docks, mooring three," The operations officer said.

"It ain't there," Banning replied.

The operations officer immediately picked up the shore to ship phone.

"Hercules, report your docking location.

"Hercules, indicate your position immediately." He repeated it several times; there was no response.

For a several seconds, there was a pause—as they tried to wrap their minds around a missing nuclear submarine—The Hercules.

The base commander ordered the entire base into lock down.

Next he ordered all available aircraft into the air to search the surrounding waters.

Then he ordered all available naval ships in the area to stop current assignments and to standby, and to immediately report in on top security lines only.

Next he ordered all ships to be queried for any visuals on the submarine Hercules. Additionally, the submarine Hercules was not to be mentioned verbally, or in written communications. Code words would be issued shortly.

Next he gave verbal instructions for a search pattern in the waters adjacent to Okinawa and ten miles out.

Then he picked up the direct line to Fleet Headquarters Honolulu, Hawaii, and muttered a prayer.

The base security officer ordered all available security personnel to be issued weapons and ordered all non-security personnel to assemble at the control tower. They formed a line and searched the entire base, perimeter to perimeter. Within an hour, they found the Okinawa gate guard covered with a camouflage blanket in the weeds near the rear gate guard shack, dead from a knife wound.

Within two hours they found a Seaman's body with a slit throat floating under a dock. His nametag read, "Baxter."

Chapter 17

DIRECTOR K WORE a blue lab coat and rubber boots because there was still a few inches of water on the floor, plus deeper puddles here and there. He smiled and shook Eddie's hand, "Good work, and everything is on schedule."

"Yes, so far," Eddie added, "They're releasing the hatches on the missile launching tubes. Your crews can start removing the Trident II missiles."

Director K pointed to the sixteen racks, each on electric mobile wheels. "We can handle all sixteen missiles, but only have enough crews to disassemble and build six units at a time. We can be completely done in seventy-two hours." Someone approached from the rear.

"Sir."

He turned his head and nodded.

"At 7:58am, there was a burst of communications from the American naval base. They have switched radio frequencies, but it's continuing," the radioman said.

"Let's get all the Trident missiles unloaded out of the Hercules, as quickly as possible.

"Admiral Yoshida, you seem worried."

Eddie looked at the Doctor of Engineering, who was a technical genius. This man had developed the technique and solved the engineering enigma of how to convert the American warheads and install them on Japanese missiles. He realized it was Director K that needed reassurance.

"Rest assured, everything is on schedule, but the entire American Navy is going to be looking for us, maybe the whole world. You follow Japanese baseball?"

"A little," Director K said.

"Good, let's stay ahead of the curve."

Eddie stood, watching as the overhead crane began lifting the 130,000 pound Trident II missile. It was slow going and it was taking too long. He wanted to complain to Director K, but caution was in order; the consequences if they dropped a missile passed through his mind. Finally, the first Trident was in the mobile rack and would soon be at ground level in the seaport dry-dock hanger for disassembly.

Eddie climbed back into the sub's control center and could see the crew moving some of the American bodies. He could also tell by the way they were struggling with the bodies that rigor was becoming a problem.

"Captain Hokan, what are you doing with the bodies?"

"We're putting them outside the sub."

"The bodies need to remain with the sub."

"Sir, they are starting to smell of death, and we are stumbling over them."

"Then you need to place the bodies where they can be easily reloaded when we get underway. Captain, put a tarp over them. I don't want to see them."

"Yes, Admiral."

Eddie thought of Ensign Crowly, who he caught as he started to fall from the sirus poison. He felt like he had killed one of his classmates from the Naval Academy. The Japanese called him Admiral Yoshida to honor him.

The Americans would have a whole bunch of names for him, and nothing honorable. He knew what he was doing was the right thing to do— it would save millions of lives—but it was the doing of it that made him feel like a murderer and traitor.

Captain Hokan Toshi was the man who would take over command of the Hercules if I became disabled. I needed to keep him advised and up-to-date on their tactics and status. Toshi was a good man and very smart. He had commanded a sub in the Japanese defense forces. He knew the risk China posed. He was still raising his three children when he was recruited by the Japanese intelligence service.

"Captain Hokan," Eddie said.

"Sir."

"Let's review where we are at and what needs to be done."

"The American communication burst occurred at 7:58 this morning. This indicates they discovered the Hercules is missing. I feel confident that they don't know where we are."

"How could they? We hid under that noisy freighter with the noise generators. Our reactor was shut down when we slipped from under the freighter into the cavern." Captain Hokan said.

"That's good, but let me explain a little about the American operations. The importance of the time delay before the Hercules was reported missing: first, that we could escape the harbor. The second important reason was so the Americans wouldn't start randomly recording everything they heard with their sonar systems. If they were recording, they could track us."

"Even under the freighter?" Inoue said.

"Yes, they would take the recordings and feed them into a computer and separate the signals. They don't have that capability in the Pacific command, but NASA does in Washington. It would take a while, maybe a week, but probably they would be able to distinguish Hercules's signature. They could not pick up our signature when we shut down the reactor."

"Then they don't know where we are?" Captain Hokan said.

"This is true, as long as we hide in this cavern. As long as we don't start the reactor, they won't know where we are. Their sonar will now be listening and recording throughout the East China Sea. We're safe for now, but shortly that luxury will pass away."

Chapter 18

Honolulu, Hawaii

THE CALL ON the direct headquarters top security line went
to Executive Officer Harley, and he nearly fainted. "Hold tight,
Captain, I'm passing you on to Rear Admiral Joyce." He walked
into Joyce's office. "Dick, you need to take this call."

Dick was not happy being interrupted in the middle of his
morning paperwork, but one look at Harley's face and he pushed
the conference call button, "Admiral Joyce."

"This is Commander Drake, Okinawa, Naval support base.
Sir, I'm reporting, I have a missing Nuclear Submarine—The
Hercules. Sir, additionally, I have three dead personnel: an Ensign
Jr. Grade, one petty officer, and a Seaman 3rd Class. We're not
sure what caused their deaths, but all three of them were manning
the Gate Control Tower on the midnight shift."

"How the fuck could this happen?" He paused. "Never mind
that, what actions have you taken?"

Commander Drake started to speak. "Stop there," Joyce said.

"Admiral Williams, you need to hear this."

Before the words had cleared his mouth, Admiral Williams
stood in his office.

"Commander Drake, repeat your entire conversation."

His voice was weaker than before.

"Admiral Williams, I'm reporting, I have a missing Nuclear Submarine—The Hercules. Sir, additionally, I have three dead personnel: an Ensign Jr. Grade, one petty officer, and a Seaman 3rd Class. We're not sure what caused their deaths, but all three of them were manning the Gate Control Tower on the midnight shift."

"What kind of a sloppy operation you running? How the fuck could this happen? Incredible." Admiral Williams paused, and regained his composure.

"Okay, what actions have you taken?"

"I'm conducting perimeter-to-perimeter base search. All available aircraft are searching the waters surrounding Okinawa and twenty-five miles out, and all available vessels are doing a grid pattern search adjacent to Okinawa and ten miles out."

"Commander Drake, what about the communications and tracking signals and locators on the sub?"

"No communication response at all. All tracking and locator devices appear to be disabled."

"It's imperative that you establish as near as possible when the Hercules separated from its berth, and when it passed through your security control gate. Commander Drake, hear this loud and clear, this is top secret and has huge international repercussions. No one is to mention a word of this, to anyone, and we do not have a missing nuclear submarine. Do you read me loud and clear?" Admiral Williams said.

"Yes, I read you loud and clear."

"Later we will inform you of a cover story. No deaths are to be reported. Do you understand me, Commander Drake?

"Yes sir, loud and clear."

"Continue what you're doing. Keep your base on prior-one alert. Cancel all leaves, until they're interviewed by Naval

Intelligence. Immediately inform Executive Officer Harley of any additional information you find, Commander; anything."

"Yes sir," Commander Drake said.

Admiral Williams looked at Joyce and Harley.

"Start working on a plausible cover story, now! We cannot have a missing nuclear submarine. We need to put in a priority request to get the spy satellites re-positioned over Okinawa and scanning that area of the Pacific, immediately.

"Let's get a grid going to determine how far the Hercules could travel in the time allowed. Do the grid both ways: first the last time it was confirmed to be in port; secondly, what time we think it was commandeered. It would help if we knew when it was taken from port."

"Place all available aircraft in and around the East China Sea on a search pattern. Let's track every ship that passed near Okinawa last night and today.

"Get a list of the crew of the Hercules. How many were on board and who they are. Pull all their personnel records and get Lt. Commander Hank from Naval Intelligence and his group scrutinizing every record.

"Also, I want Hank to get in the back seat of a fighter jet and personally interview Commander Drake, his Security Officer, and Operations Officer today. Got that. Tell Lt. Commander Hank to get hold of me before he leaves.

"Whoever is responsible for this has a plan. You find anything at all, I want to know immediately. Leave no hatch unopened."

He walked into his office and looked at a map of the South Pacific.

"Sir, we just got more information. They found an Okinawan gate guard dead from a knife wound, and a Seaman from the Hercules, floating under a dock, dead from a slit throat," Vice Admiral Joyce said.

Admiral Williams placed one hand on each side of his head and massaged his temples.

He tried to think, who would commandeer a nuclear submarine, and why, and how did they do it? Could they have killed everyone aboard, and just stolen the sub? More likely, someone on board commandeered the sub. How many men does it take to minimally man the Hercules? Whoever did it knew how to disable the locators and pilot a nuclear sub. They were up to no good, in a big way. He swallowed two aspirins and picked up the direct line to the Pentagon.

Chapter 19

Pentagon, Washington DC

THE PHONE RANG and it was immediately picked up. "Pentagon operations."

"Admiral Williams here, I need to speak with the watch commander.

"General Hess, I have to report that we have a missing nuclear submarine. The Hercules, the submarine, was moved from its berth without authorization from the Okinawa Naval support facility. It was moved sometime after midnight last night," Admiral Williams said.

"Admiral Williams, I'm declaring this a red code four and top secret."

"Have you issued a cover story for the increased military activity in the Okinawa area?"

"Yes, General Hess, we have issued a missing Navy transport aircraft, that was en route to Okinawa."

"Admiral Williams, I have patched you through to the Joint Chief of Staff Command Center. You are now speaking to the Operations Command Center for all United States military operations throughout the world. Our conversation has already been converted to text and is on the large screen. All appropriate staff members are reading this as we speak."

"Yes, I understand."

"Who is piloting the submarine? How many navy personnel were on the Hercules when it was taken?" General Meyers said.

"We estimate there are thirty-four naval officers and men aboard the submarine Hercules. Lieutenant Woodmen was certified to pilot the submarine Hercules. If he is piloting the Hercules, I have no idea."

"Can you operate the Hercules with just thirty-four men?"

"Yes, but the problem comes when you have to run more than six hours. You will have no relief for the men manning the operating stations. You would have to shut down after eight hours."

"We now have representatives of the CIA and FBI at the commander center and they're reading the board to get up-to-date. I've also been notified that spy satellites are being repositioned to scan Okinawa and the South Pacific Ocean, but it's almost a day away before it will be area operational. Plus, the Joint Chiefs of Staff have ordered a review of all communications in and around Okinawa, for the last 30 days from the National Security Agency. We have now been joined by the Secretary of Defense Hart."

"Is there any way the nuclear missiles can be fired?" Secretary Hart said.

"Sir, there is no way those missiles can be fired. It requires a code from Pacific Fleet Headquarters and Naval operations Norfolk. Plus a matching code stored aboard the vessel, accessible by the submarine's commander," Admiral Williams said.

"I understand what you're saying, but why commandeer a nuclear submarine with sixteen nuclear missiles unless you have a plan to utilize the weapons?" Secretary Hart said.

"I understand what you mean, Mr. Secretary, but they won't be able to crack the code."

"I have an uneasy feeling about not being able to break the code," Secretary Hart replied.

Chapter 20

White House, DC

THE PRESIDENT SAT at his desk and listened as the Joint Chief of Staff and the Secretary of Defense informed him of the disappearance of the nuclear submarine Hercules.

"How could this have happened, General Meyers?"

"Mr. President, we're reviewing all security on submarine Naval bases. But this was a well-thought out and well-executed plan."

"General, the American taxpayer pays of billions of dollars every month to support the military. Now you're telling me that someone snuck onto one of our Naval bases and stole our most capable nuclear submarine."

"We have all Naval submarine bases on alert, and they have added extra security for the submarines," Secretary Hart said.

"We need to recover, or at least discover what has happened to this missing nuclear submarine and within a few days. Protocol requires that I inform the Japanese; it's their island, after all. I cannot wait more than three days.

"I would appreciate you finding the Hercules before then. It would be incredibly humiliating if the Hercules appears in some foreign harbor—with only God knows who will be aboard. Do you know what an embarrassment this is?" President Warde said.

"I have ordered all submarines not on patrol to proceed at top speed into the East China Sea. If the Hercules is operating in that area, we will find it. Every submarine has a distinct noise. It's called a signature, and we have the Hercules's on file. Every submarine searching that area will be comparing sonar sounds to that signature. If it moves, we will find it." Secretary Hart said.

"About eighteen months ago we developed and installed a sonar and hydrophone defense system south and east of Guam to protect our forces from a foreign sub getting right on top of us. That network has not detected a sub moving towards Guam. I believe the Hercules is still in the East China Sea because not enough time has passed for the Hercules to cruise out of the East China Sea. The only way it could have gotten out would be if it were running at top speed, but the sound and signature would have been detected by the Guam sonar defense system."

"In another twelve hours, we will have enough submarines strategically positioned to prevent the Hercules from leaving the East China Sea. At the very least it will allow us to detect the Hercules by its signature as it tries to flee." General Meyers said.

"Would it help if I asked Japanese Prime Minister Okada to deploy the Japanese Naval defense force?"

"Mr. President, I think we should keep this an American operation and under wraps as long as possible. A commandeered nuclear submarine is not something to instill confidence in our ability to recover it. Truthfully, we still don't know who is behind this."

"General Meyer, you're probably right, but we don't have a lot of time. I cannot in good conscience fail to inform our allies in that area of Asia, after more than a few days. I want to be kept informed."

Chapter 21

East China Sea

THE JAPANESE SUBMERSIBLE missiles looked much like the American Tridents outer casings. But all labeling was in Japanese and the internal controls, as well as all communications equipment, were Japanese.

The American Trident II missile weighed 130,000 lbs. It could travel more than 4,000 miles at a speed in excess of 13,600 mph. The Japanese submersible missile was developed over four years, in secret. It was a fourth the size of the American Trident II, and its speed only in excess of 2,000 mph, and its range limited to 1,500 miles. It was designed to carry three nuclear warheads. The Japanese had no nuclear warheads. It was developed almost exclusively as protection against Chinese aggression.

It was a submersible design and water-tight, but filled with nitrogen to keep moisture out. Its weight of 28,000 pounds was a necessity so it could be fired from stand-alone missile launching stations sitting on the ocean bottom. When the launching station was activated, it would rise to within 200 feet of the water's surface. The tube containing the missile would elevate to an eighty-five degree angle before ignition. When the missile broke the surface and entered the atmosphere, navigational systems would take control.

The sixteen missiles were slowly hauled up to the ground above. They came to rest in a large industrial building that was used for repairing the mammoth engines, cranes, and industrial elevators of the ocean-going freighters. Outside, the docks were busy, day and night, as Japanese dock workers loaded and unloaded shipping containers, automobiles, industrial construction vehicles, and lots of other cargoes. Additionally, freight was moved in and out of storage, as loads were consolidated.

"Lt. Ito, as soon as the tridents are cleared out of the Hercules, get the American communications equipment disconnected. Put the American equipment in the electronics storage locker. Then install the Japanese communications equipment sitting on these two pallets to the Hercules antennas."

"Yes, understood," Lt. Ito said.

The Japanese technicians waiting for the Trident II missiles quickly got to work. Inside the warehouse, they began disassembly of the first six missiles. The Trident's three warheads were to be mated with a single Japanese submersible launching station.

"Admiral Yoshida, there is an unexpected design change in the American coupling that holds the three warheads in position. It's only a slight change, but still we have to modify it before it can be used in our stand-alone launching unit."

"How much time will it take?"

"I'm not sure, but I will personally redesign the coupling."

Within two hours, Director K had designed the new coupling and had blueprints ready for the industrial machinist, and resin for the chemist to compound.

Using an industrial laser pattern cutter and a lathe, the new coupling would modify the trident coupling and allow it to function inside the Japanese stand-alone launching unit. It had to be made of aluminum and coated with a plastic resin. This was to prevent aluminum and copper creating corrosion when in contact with each other. But it took time—too much time—four hours to manufacturer each coupling.

Eddie stood with Captain Hokan looking at the latest reconnaissance information from the Japanese spy satellite. It had been a little more than thirty-six hours since the American Nuclear Submarine Hercules had been commandeered. The sky was filled with American planes searching, and spy satellites scanning everything.

"Everything is concentrated on the East China Sea. Why?" Captain Hokan said.

"Somehow they know we didn't get out of the East China Sea."

"But they don't know where we are," Captain Hokan said.

"The American Navy is betting that they have us bottled up in the East China Sea."

They saw Director K approaching and he looked worried.

He bowed.

"I am humbly sorry. We should have had eight launching stations ready for deployment. We only have four. In four hours, we will have another two units available," Director K said.

"I understand. I know you have done your best. But we must change our tactics to accommodate the time delay. The important point is to accomplish this mission." Eddie said.

"Yes, I understand," the Director said.

"We need to load the four finished launching stations on the freighter immediately. Your oceanographer and Captain Hokan will deploy the launching stations," Eddie said.

"Admiral Yoshida, I should remain with the Hercules. You need me," Captain Hokan said.

"It's more important that the launching stations get deployed—even four stations. Just having the launching stations does us no good. They must be deployed and ready to launch

before we have an effective nuclear deterrent. Captain, you know
where the Americans ships are arrayed and how their sonar works.
Dr. Risa, the oceanographer and yourself must select new sites
along the route that the freighter is taking to Yokomo. She will
select the site and you must make the launching stations' entry into
the ocean as silently as possible."

Captain Hokan knew an order when he heard one.

"Admiral Yoshida, it will be as you say."

"The noise made by the entry of the launching station into the
water and its descent to the ocean floor will not be the kind of
sound the Americans will be listening for. However, you want to
keep it as noiseless as possible because you don't want to make
them curious enough to investigate," Eddie said.

Later, Eddie watched from the window inside the repair
compound. He dared not go outside with the American satellites
sweeping overhead, recording everything. He watched the
mammoth iron-ore carrier, bearing the flag of the Philippines but
manned by Japanese sailors, slowly move away from the docks. It
would take six days before it reached its destination of Yokohama,
Japan. Concealed on its bottom deck were four launching stations.
The massive hull of the ship provided cover for the deployment of
the stations into the East China Sea, and within 250 miles of the
Chinese coast.

In a few days, and before the Philippine cargo vessel reached
the port at Yokohama, Japan would have deployed four nuclear-
missile-launching stations. The Japanese Naval defense force would
have its own nuclear weapons under its command, to protect its
homeland. In another week's time, they would have a total of
sixteen single-missile nuclear launching stations strategically
positioned. Japan would have a formidable nuclear deterrent
against anyone within the limits of the missiles' modest fuel range.
Specifically on everyone's mind was the Red Star of China. All
sixteen launching stations could hit the coastal area of China, plus

almost thirteen hundred miles inland. Thus, they could target all of China's strategic military bases, and key industrial complexes, and cities.

Chapter 22

Honolulu, Hawaii

WITHIN FORTY-EIGHT HOURS, the American submarines had established listening posts surrounding the East China Sea. Anti-submarine aircraft patrolled the skies and two aircraft carriers anchored the south and north ends of the South China Sea … Their decks were busy refueling anti-submarine and patrol aircraft.

"I want anti-submarine aircraft in the air searching twenty-four hours a day until we find the Hercules; make sure Admiral Rogers knows that. Tell him to scrub missions, and pull pilots from other tasks to help with the flying. Use only anti-submarine aircraft. It's the only chance we have of detecting the Hercules. The other aircraft will just fly over the sub and won't have a chance of detecting it." Admiral Williams said.

White House, Washington DC

The president sat at his desk with two hands holding up his right knee, as he leaned back in his chair. "Well, General Meyers, where are we at?"

General Meyers pointed at the map with a laser pointer in his hand.

He then used his laser to highlight the position of the American submarines and their listening capabilities. Then using the laser in a circular motion he indicated the patterns being flown by Naval anti-submarine aircraft.

"Mr. President, we have the submarine Hercules boxed in the East China Sea, there's no way they can move that sub around without one of our ships picking up their signature."

"What is the Hercules doing if it's not moving?"

"It's probably lying on the bottom of the ocean using minimum equipment to avoid detection. I'm sure they're hoping we will reduce the number of ships and aircraft we have patrolling, so they can slip past our perimeter."

"Douglas Hammar is here from the CIA, let's listen to what he has to say," The President said.

"We've identified a group of Japanese paramilitary operating under several different names. Basically, they have advocated arming Japan with nuclear weapons for a number of years because China has nuclear weapons. They feel it's the only way to protect Japan from the Chinese, which they consider to be an ancient and deadly foe."

"Japan is protected under the American nuclear umbrella agreement," General Meyer said.

Everyone ignored the Generals' comment.

"As you're probably aware all senior American military officers are required to register with the department of defense if they reside outside the United States when they retire. I had our staff review all senior military retirees living in Japans and Southeast Asia.

"They found an American Naval officer that raised several red flags. He is residing in Tokyo, Japan, he barely qualifies as a high ranking officer. But because of his Naval career and the commandeering of the nuclear submarine Hercules, he drew the interest of our staff. Here is a copy of his service record."

He reached into his briefcase and dropped it on the table.

"What I found most interesting is that he was the Hercules's engineering officer on its shakedown voyage. Later he was the skipper for a three-year tour. If retired Captain Eddie Yoshida is implicated in this, he knows the Hercules, the Pacific, and Naval operating procedures inside and out."

"Save me some reading. What else?" The President said.

"He's a graduate of Annapolis Naval Academy and retired from the Navy after twenty-three years' service. He retired with the rank of Captain. Most of his career was spent in the submarine service. Eddie's wife died of cancer about five years before he retired from the Navy. A couple years later he remarried a Japanese women name of Kaori, they have two children they reside in a suburb of Tokyo. They have lived there for more than six years. Eddie, because his wife is a Japanese citizen, has dual citizenship.

"We began trying to contact Eddie Yoshida immediately after reviewing his military record. We haven't been able to reach him or his wife. Our agents in Japan visited their home, but no one is there and no one is answering their phones. We have left messages—but no response. His wife is a professor at Tokyo University and we made an inquiry at the University. We were informed that Professor Kaori Yoshida and her family are on a secluded Buddhist retreat and can't be contacted. In short, we don't know where Eddie Yoshida and his family are."

"What's your gut feeling?" The president said.

"All the information these pirates needed to commandeer the Hercules, Captain Yoshida possessed. We have tried to contact him, but he has conveniently disappeared. Did Captain Yoshida do it voluntary? Was he coerced? I don't know. But yes—he's definitely involved."

"That explains a lot. He knows our nuclear submarines, our operating procedures, and our tactics. I'm sure he knew the Naval Support Base at Okinawa rather well. He is a retired Naval commander and he took a lifelong oath. He is nothing less than a traitor, to his oath, to the Navy, his fellow officers, and his country," Secretary Hart said.

"Retired Captain Eddie would know how to lie on the ocean floor and avoid detection. But sooner or later they have to do something, and eventually their air supply will need replenishing, and they will have to activate the reactor. An experienced submarine commander, or not, we still have them boxed in. It doesn't change our procedure. They don't have the codes to fire the missiles," General Meyers said.

"Something about this doesn't sound right. Why commandeer a nuclear submarine if you don't have a plan," Secretary Hart said.

"Pressure from the Tokyo police might have forced them to act before they were entirely ready," Hammar said.

"What does the Japanese government know about this paramilitary group?" The President said.

"We have a reliable source within the Tokyo police force who passed this info to our agent in Tokyo. The Japanese security service has been hunting this paramilitary gang for the last three months, but mostly for weapons violations," Hammar said.

"Is our cover story about a missing Naval transport aircraft still holding up?" Secretary Hart said.

"Yes, but there's a hell of a lot of activity in the East China Sea and I'm sure other countries are taking notice, but no inquiries, so far," General Meyers said.

"We have been notified by NSA that the Japanese have repositioned one of their satellites so it passes directly over Okinawa and the East China Sea," Hammar said.

"Gentleman we're running out of time. I must soon notify our allies in the East that we have a missing nuclear submarine. It's almost three days. I can't delay much longer."

"If we could hold off another twenty-four hours, we might just get a break," Secretary Hart said.

"I certainly hope so," the President said.

Chapter 23

White House, Washington DC

"IT'S BEEN FOUR days. I have to inform our Southeast Asia allies that we have a missing nuclear submarine before they find out some other way, and I am the last one to inform them," the President said.

"Are we going to say it was commandeered, or only missing?" Secretary Hart said.

"We don't have to tell the same story to all the allies. Only as much as they need to know, and we will have fulfilled our obligation of notification," General Meyer said.

"The Japanese know everything. They also suspect that the Renegade group commandeered the Hercules. They haven't told us what they know, but their security service has been chasing the Renegades for months," Hammar said.

"Okay, we level with the Japanese. South Korea, Philippines, and China, we only state we have a missing nuclear submarine. It's been gone for more than seventy-two hours. We are unsure about what has happened to it, but believe it's in the East China Sea and we have a massive search operation in progress. There is absolutely no way that the nuclear missiles can be launched without Naval

Headquarters Washington, DC providing the arming codes for the missiles."

"Mr. President, Japanese Prime Minister Okada is ready to receive your call."

The President picked up the red phone.

"Good day, Prime Minister Okada. I hope you're having a pleasant day. I'm calling to inform you that our Pacific fleet has a missing nuclear submarine—the Hercules. We are conducting a vast search operation throughout the East China Sea. We are unsure how the Hercules was taken from our Naval support base in Okinawa, but a complete investigation is underway. I want to assure you that the nuclear missiles cannot be activated without receiving dual encrypted coding from Naval Headquarters. We find this very alarming and are doing everything we can to resolve this situation as quickly as possible."

"President Warde, what can the Japanese government do to assist you?"

"Nothing right now. But I would appreciate any help you can give Douglas Hammar, the head of our CIA. He is investigating a group of Japanese called the Renegades. Also, he is trying to make contact with a retired American Naval officer. His name is Eddie Yoshida. He is married to a Japanese women and lives in Tokyo. It's possible he may have something to do with the missing Hercules."

"I will have the head of our National Security Agency contact him."

*****

"Chinese Prime Minister Li Wei is ready to receive your call."

President Warde picked up the red phone.

"Good day, Prime Minister Li. I hope you're having a pleasant day. I'm calling to inform you that our Pacific fleet has a missing nuclear submarine, the Hercules. We are conducting a vast search operation in the East China Sea. We are unsure what has happened, but we have a complete investigation underway. Additionally, I want to assure you that the nuclear missiles cannot be activated without receiving dual encrypted coding from Naval Headquarters. We find this situation very alarming and are doing everything we can to resolve this situation as quickly as possible."

"Our people's defense forces have noticed an increase in your Naval and air activity in the East China Sea. It appears to be a massive search operation. Tell me, Mr. President, what is implied by the term 'missing nuclear submarine?'"

"Li, I'm unsure of all the details."

"Why then did you feel that you had to reassure me that the nuclear missiles cannot be fired?"

"I'm just trying to allay any fears you might have."

"If the submarine has crashed you wouldn't have to worry about nuclear missiles being fired. Are you saying this Hercules is operational, but not responding to US military authority?"

"Prime Minister Li, I'm unsure about the details."

"One more question, President Warde. When did this occur?"

"Approximately three days ago. Prime Minister Li, I will keep you informed. Thank you for your understanding."

He looked at Secretary Hart.

"That wasn't easy. Prime Minister Li is suspicious. He suspects I'm not forthright, and there is a lot more to this than I have told him. We have got to get this resolved, and quickly. You need to light a fire under General Meyers."

"Yes, Mr. President, I will."

Chapter 24

Tokyo, Japan

PRIME MINISTER OKADA sat thinking about the call from President Warde. He looked at Sato, who had read the words, as they were spoken, on a computer screen. "What do you think Sato?"

"I don't think the Americans are blaming us yet. But they did inquire about the Renegades, and about Eddie Yoshida, my brother-in-law."

"They are only inquiring about the Renegades because we fed their CIA information through their Tokyo police informative. But where did they get Eddie Yoshida's name?" Okada said.

"Eddie is a senior Naval officer and has to keep his residence registered with the American Navy. Eddie didn't know if they would check on him. But as a precaution we moved his family and created a cover story that they are on a secluded Buddhist retreat."

"That's good."

"He didn't take your offer of deploying our Naval forces to assist the Americans."

"Why should they? The American's have all the naval vessels they need. Plus, they feel they have the Hercules bottled up in the

East China Sea. Our meager Navy would just be in the way. No, they want an exclusive American operation," Okada said.

"Then the Americans don't know what to think—they're still looking for evidence," Sato said.

The Prime Minister got out of his chair and began pacing the floor—he didn't like deceiving President Warde.

"Yes, I think you're correct," Okada said.

Beijing, China

Prime Minister Li Wei hung up the phone and was already fuming. He could sense the President of the United States wasn't being truthful; a missing nuclear submarine. A nuclear submarine that has not disabled and is lying at the bottom of the ocean. No, what he meant was, it's not responding to American Naval commands. Who would want a nuclear submarine with nuclear missiles aboard? He scowled. The fucking Japs.

He picked up the phone and told Wang Yong, head of military intelligence, to come to his office. "What do we know about a missing American nuclear submarine?"

"We know the Americans are conducting a massive search operation in the East China Sea. Additionally, we've heard a rumor, but it is unconfirmed, that the American nuclear submarine called the 'Hercules' was discovered missing from its berth at the American Naval base in Okinawa. Additionally, there is a Japanese paramilitary group that is suspected to be deeply involved. But this is all unconfirmed."

"Do we know anything else?"

"No," Wang said.

"Who would want an American nuclear submarine?" Li said.

"The Japanese."

"Why?"

"It would give them a nuclear deterrent if they could operate the American nuclear submarine. I'm not sure how the American missile launch authorization works. But I would think that it would take two authorizations, one from the submarine commander and one from higher command. It's possible they wanted to grab the sub and duplicate the best and latest technology," Yong said.

"I think an instant nuclear deterrent is most plausible. That means the Japanese don't trust the Americans to honor their nuclear umbrella commitment if they get in a squabble with us over some islands."

"Prime Minister, I think that is very true."

"Do everything possible to find more information on the American missing nuclear sub, and I want that information as quickly as possible."

"Yes, immediately," Yong said.

Chapter 25

Beijing, China

PRIME MINISTER LI Wei called together a meeting of the Politburo Standing Committee. He sat in the committee meeting room looking at the five members.

"I received a call from President Warde this morning. He informed me that the American Pacific fleet has a nuclear submarine missing. He assures me that its payload of nuclear missiles cannot be launched. I asked him if the nuclear submarine had crashed to the bottom of the sea. He responded that he was unsure of the details and that it went missing three days ago."

"Wang Yong, the head of military intelligence, told me that the Americans have initiated a massive search operation and that it is concentrated in the East China Sea. This started four days ago. The Americans have flooded the East China Sea with anti-submarine aircraft and ships, and submarines. The truth appears to be that this nuclear submarine was taken from its berth at the American Naval station in Okinawa. Yong also reported a rumor that a Japanese paramilitary group has reportedly commandeered the American nuclear submarine. Yong believes that the story will prove to be true."

"Tell us what you are thinking, Li," Wang Lei said.

"I think Prime Minister Okada is behind the commandeering of the American nuclear submarine. They know the Americans will not risk a nuclear exchange to defend a few islands. So they grabbed the American submarine to try and duplicate the technology, or it's an attempt to crack the American missiles codes. President Warde assured me that the American launch systems require two authorizations; one aboard ship and the other from a higher command."

"What is it you want to do about this situation?" Wang Lei said.

"I want to take the two islands that we are in dispute with from Japan, plus the island of Kume."

"How do you proposal to justify that?" Wang Lei said.

"After we secure them we will issue a statement that the islands in dispute were ours to begin with, and reference our eighteenth century Mariner's maps. The last island we have taken in retribution for the destruction of the Three Gorges Dam. We will send the inhabitants back to Japan, where they belong."

"What of the America treaty with Japan?" Li Qiang said.

"The Japanese would not have commandeered the American submarine if they thought the Americans would honor the treaty. Prime Minister Okada has tipped his hand by grabbing the American submarine. He knows the Americans will not be drawn into a war over three islands. He needs a nuclear deterrent and he doesn't have one."

"What about the missiles on the nuclear submarine?" Li Jun said.

"I believe that the American launch codes cannot be cracked; also you need an authorization code from higher command. I think the Japanese stole the American sub to duplicate the technology and create a deterrent, but it will take time. We need to move now."

"How would you move, Prime Minister LI?" Li Jun said.

"I think we should have North Korea fire one of their long-range missiles over Japan and see how they react. The Americans would not respond over a harmless missile passing over Japanese airspace. The Japanese won't like it, but the Americans will not react.

"If the Japanese are incensed, they will respond and show what weapons they have. Then we can come to the aid of our friends in North Korea. World opinion will be on our side. Plus, we have the outrage over the destruction of the Three Gorges Dam.

"I am going to act quickly before the Japanese so-called paramilitary gang can create any problems with the American nuclear submarine." Prime Minister Li Wei turned and left the room.

The five members of the Standing Committee of the Politburo looked at each other.

"What is Li Wei doing?" Chang said.

"I don't feel like I've been consulted. We don't know if Japan did anything—Li's going to get us in a war," Li Jun said.

"Maybe a war with the Americans. We need to have a meeting tomorrow tonight," Wang Lei said.

Chapter 26

East China Sea

EDDIE YOSHIDA ASSEMBLED the men who had arrived on the Hercules in the cavern; there were forty-four men in total.

"So far our mission has been accomplished. The additional time it has taken to assemble the warheads onto our missiles has been very costly. The Americans have surrounded the East China Sea and have woven a very tight net of sonar listening stations. It will be very difficult to escape this tight net, but we must try, and in the process fool the American Navy.

"The Americans believe the Hercules is lying on the ocean floor, and we are waiting for them to stop their search, or remove vessels from their perimeter listening posts. Then they suspect the Hercules will attempt to pass through their perimeter undetected.

"Soon the American Navy will have enough ships in the area that they can man the perimeter and begin an underwater search. It won't be long before the American commanders begin to question their assumption that we are lying on the ocean floor, playing a waiting game. If their sonar doesn't detect noise soon, then they will begin a very thorough search for the Hercules, especially around islands, looking for anything out of the ordinary, and any place the Hercules could be hiding. If they start searching with their sophisticated electronics and sonar, they will find this underwater cavern.

"If this cavern is discovered, it will have disastrous consequences. Japan would be forced to surrender the American warheads and this would leave Japan defenseless again Chinese nuclear weapons.

"It would be humiliating and a significant loss of face if Japan were caught with the American submarine Hercules and held responsible for the death of thirty-four American submariners. The American people would be outraged.

"Japan would lose its American support. This support is vital until Japan has its own nuclear weapons deployed and ready for use. For a little while longer, we need the illusion of the American nuclear umbrella to keep the Chinese hesitant to attack Japan.

"Lt. Ito and I have planned an escape in the opposite direction of the East China Sea, but it is fraught with risk and could fail. If we cannot escape, then it's imperative that the Hercules not be allowed to fall back into the hands of the Americans.

"If our escape routes are cut off, then we must pilot the Hercules into the deepest depths of the Pacific, the Mariana Trench, on a one-way voyage. When the ocean depth is at least three miles or deeper, the Hercules will dive to such a depth that the pressure will crush the submarine. Then it will sink to one of the lowest depths in the entire Pacific ocean. This way the Americans will never be able to recover the Hercules and never know for sure if the warheads are missing.

"You will be crushed to death by the force of the ocean's water pressure. As for me, I will not be crushed to death but will perform Hara-kiri just before the walls of the submarine start to collapse. It is my honored duty to do this for my ancestors, my family, and Japan.

"Now, of the forty-four men standing here, I'm asking for eighteen men to volunteer. This is enough to minimally man the Hercules as we attempt our escape. Those who want to volunteer, step forward one step."

All forty-four sailors stepped forward. He had somehow expected this to happen. Now, he asked all single men without families to step forward. There were more than twenty. He slowly walked down the line of sailors and tapped eighteen men on the shoulder.

He walked back up front.

"Then, this is how it will be. The rest of you, who will be leaving on the freighter back to Japan, remember these men. You must take what you have seen, what you have done, to the grave with you, and not a word of this must ever pass your lips. You sons of Japan have done your duty. Japan is proud of you. Go now, you are dismissed."

He saluted them, as they saluted him.

Chapter 27

East China Sea

THE TRIDENT MISSILES had been loaded back into the Hercules's missile launch tubes, minus the nuclear warheads. He wanted everything in place, in the event the Hercules was ever viewed by remote cameras, lying on the bottom in very deep water. *We must buy Japan as much time as possible.*

He stood in the control and attack center watching the eighteen volunteers as they began climbing down the ladder. He had mixed emotions, proud of them, and sad their lives might end so early. *Eddie muttered to himself, we live again and again, which he sincerely believed.*

He watched as the bodies of the American submariners were brought aboard. He couldn't allow the bodies to be placed in body bags. It was a gruesome task. He asked Lt. Ito to assist him, and together they stacked the bodies as they were slid through the door into the cramped quarters of the accessory supply compartment. He laid Ensign Crowly on top of four other bodies, then looked at his swollen face and blue eyes. He latched the door, sealing in the horrible smell of death. For a couple of minutes, he felt shame and guilt, as he wondered, *what have I done.*

Still, the smell of death lingered. He went to the skipper's quarters and showered. He dressed, but the smell wouldn't go away; he removed his clothes; he looked in the skipper's wardrobe and changed into a commander's uniform that was close to his size.

"Admiral Yoshida, if I may speak."

Eddie nodded his head.

"Sir, it is not necessary for you to go on this voyage. My family is raised, and the loss of my life is not so important. Admiral, you could be of great service to Japan. I could pilot the sub. If the attempt to escape is unsuccessful, then I take Hercules on its last voyage."

"Lt. Ito, I understand what you are saying. Only you and I are capable of piloting and navigating this huge submarine. If I become disabled, you must fulfill the mission. What if you became disabled? The Hercules cannot be allowed to fall back into American hands. If that happens, then our mission will have failed. All the lives lost will be for nothing. Japan will be lost."

Eddie told the radioman to notify Director K to relay the signal to the Japanese fishing boat. The message was sent that turned on the first recording of the Hercules signature.

He climbed up to the open hatch of the sail and watched pumps in reverse, hard at work filling the cave with seawater. They had to fill the cave before opening the door to equalize the pressure so the massive door could open. He ordered the hatch closed and looked at the remote camera screen as the cavern filled with seawater. He waited for the signal that the massive cavern door was fully open.

The red diode lit up and there was tapping from the divers on the hatch. The mechanical arm assists were in place and cavern door was open. He could feel the mechanical arms slowly nudging the Hercules. He ordered a little water jettisoned from the ballasts to give the Hercules a bit of buoyancy. A few minutes later the green diode lit and again he heard tapping at the sail hatch. They had cleared the cave's entrance.

He ordered Lt. Ito to bring the Hercules to six-degree downward angle using battery power, and to proceed 4.3 nautical miles. That should put them very close to the horizontal surface on a ridge rising from the ocean's floor. Twenty-one minutes later the Hercules rested on the rim of a plateau rising almost five hundred above the ocean floor.

"Lt. Ito, the Americans are responding to the recording," the radioman said.

"They are tired of waiting, and eager for action," Lt. Ito said.

"They have taken the bait," Eddie said.

He waited another half hour before instructing the radioman to message for the second recording to be activated. It was almost two hundred nautical miles away from the first recording.

It was forty minutes later when they got an encrypted signal—the Americans were responding to the second recording, too.

Now it was time to address the crew. He pushed the intercom button.

"Now we make our move. In five minutes time we will crank up the reactor, then slowly increase our speed to fourteen knots. We will maintain a depth of seven hundred feet. This is the speed and depth at which the Hercules signature was recorded. This way all the signatures the Americans are picking up will sound the same. Let's keep them confused, for as long as possible."

They slowly cranked up the reactor, lifted off the plateau, and increased the Hercules speed to fourteen knots. Eddie envisioned the skippers aboard submarines manning listening posts throughout the East China Sea. The crews would be cheering once they heard the noise, and even more excited once they identified the Hercules's signature. Of course, they now had three identical signatures to chase after as they tried to guess which one was real.

"Lt. Ito, make way for the Babuyan Islands. Set a direct course and get as much distance as we can while the Americans are confused. In another forty minutes time, I will signal for the third recorded signature transmitter to be activated."

"Petty Officer Hito, after the food supplies are stored, arrange rotating shifts of twelve men on duty and six men off. Rotate every six hours," Lt. Ito said.

They were almost an hour into cruising at fourteen knots when Eddie sent the message to Director K to relay the command to turn on the last recorded signature transmitter. It, too, was located almost two hundred nautical miles from the previous recorder. Now the Naval commanders had four signals to choose from, all two hundred nautical miles apart, and chasing these would spread the American fleet thin.

Eddie spoke on the intercom.

"We are making way for the Babuyan Islands in the Philippines archipelago. That's approximately seven hundred nautical miles, and our estimated cruising time is thirty-two hours. Use the intercom for communicating."

"Admiral Yoshida, there is an encrypted signal the Americans are responding to—the third recorded signature transmitter," the radio operator said.

Eddie lay in the skipper's bunk near the command center and closed his eyes, but sleep wouldn't come. Images and words kept floating through his mind. His first wife, dead for more than ten years, would never have moved to Japan. After her death, he was free to go to Japan, and he did. He met Karoi at a Buddhist meeting; she was a part-time professor at Tokyo University, and now they had two children.

Karoi had introduced him to her sister's husband, Sato, who was Minister of Defense under Prime Minister Kato. His wife and her sister, and especially Sato, felt the threat from China was real. They often discussed whether the Americans would protect Japan's islands under their nuclear umbrella agreement. Eddie's answer was honest and forthright. "I honestly don't think they would. But if the Chinese acted rashly, it is possible the American military would react before the public had a chance to voice their opposition."

He tried to sleep, but the image of Ensign Crowly floated to the surface of his mind. Again he saw him breathing in sirus gas and caught him as he fell. Once more he stepped over his comatose body, as he lay on the deck, still breathing but unconscious. Again he stood watching as Ensign Crowly slowly suffocated to death. A plan on paper is so different from the actual killing of someone. To be there—to touch the person you killed. He had killed thirty-four American submariners—his countrymen. He closed his eyes but could still feel the decaying flesh as he lifted their bodies.

In his heart, he knew what he did was right but, only his wife and Japan would see it that way. If it prevented a nuclear exchange between America and China, it was worth it. Of course, it was possible no one would ever find out about his betrayal. He hoped so—it was not his proudest moment.

A depiction of Benedict Arnold being searched at a roadblock floated into his mind. A traitor who tried to convey Washington's battle plans to the British. *Arnold had never even killed anyone. Arnold would look like a saint compared to me; I stole a nuclear submarine, killed thirty-four crew members and betrayed my oath, my fellow officers, and my country.*

He could still smell the scent of death on his hands. He got up and washed his hands with soap and water. Then lay on the bunk again and drifted off to a disturbed sleep.

Eddie awoke six hours later.

"Admiral Yoshida you need to listen to this," the radio operator said.

He placed the earphones over his ears and heard the pinging noise.

"When did it start?"

"About five minutes ago."

"The same sonar ping?"

"Yes."

"Let me know when you hear a different ping noise."

"Yes, Sir."

Lt. Ito poured some tea out of thermoses and handed it to Eddie.

"You must have been tired."

"I guess I was. Can't believe I slept six hours."

"What do you make of the ping?"

"I'm sure they're pinging all four locations."

"But recordings don't send echoes back."

"Eventually they will figure out we're the Hercules and not a recording. So it's a race for us to get to the Babuyan Islands before they find us. They have to figure out where we are going and how to cut us off," Eddie said.

"Lt. Ito, you need to get some sleep, too."

"Admiral, you don't have to tell me twice."

Eddie watched Ito walk towards the cot and thought, *he will be asleep before he hits the mattress, lucky guy.*

Eddie sat in the commander's chair, thinking. *They were nine hours into their escape run and had a decent chance of pulling it off. He had not been that optimistic about fooling the Americans for so long. He guessed they wanted to be extremely thorough in identifying each of the Hercules's recorded signature transmissions, even if it required tracking down recordings. The Pacific Command would be under enormous pressure to make no mistakes and to be dead sure not to let the Hercules escape.*

"Admiral Yoshida, I have cooked eggs, rice and egg roll," Seaman Ren said.

He had a plastic tray in his hands.

"Lt. Ito said you would prefer to eat out here."

"Yes, I do. Thanks."

He looked at the seaman and thought him to be about twenty years old.

"Seaman Ren, how long have you been a submariner?"

"Sir, three years active Navy with two years of that in the submarine service, and then a reservist."

"You're a good cook."

"First-time, Admiral. I have never cooked on a sub before. This is how I cook at home."

"What made you want to be a submariner?"

"My grandfather and my father were submariners and they told interesting stories, and it made me want to be a submariner. My grandfather survived the war."

"Admiral, was your ..." Ren stopped.

"No, we were on the American side. My father was in an internment camp in California. The American government didn't trust us."

They looked at each other, then started laughing. Maybe it was because they were in a stolen American sub, and the tension; but they laughed hard.

Eddie poured some soy sauce on his rice and eggs; it was delicious. Then he poured more tea. He looked at his watch; it was twelve hours since they departed the cavern. Up top, dawn would soon be breaking.

He felt refreshed after some sleep, good food, and hot tea.

He wondered what this day held in store.

"Admiral, I'm getting another noise, but I can't identify it."

Eddie put the earphones over his ears and listened, but there were no sounds.

"What did it sound like?"

"Sort of like a weak ping but much shorter in duration?"

Eddie handed him the headphones.

"Place your radio on audio and headphones. That way we will hear it together."

It was almost an hour before they heard a series of short pings. They stopped as suddenly as they had begun. The radioman looked at him.

"Sir that was the sound I heard before."

"That is a sonar ping from an anti-submarine aircraft flying off one of the American aircraft carriers."

Eddie thought, *they're still uncertain or that aircraft would be circling back, trying to get a better reading. The ping is not returning to their sonar system, or it's delayed, and they can't pinpoint our location. They may try to drop sonobuoys and triangulate on our position.*

If I dive deeper, I won't sound like the other recordings. It is possible they have already determined that the other Hercules signatures were fake; or maybe not. I'll wait and see if it circles back.

Eddie thought about the Japanese radio and encrypting equipment and felt sure the Americans wouldn't suspect them of communicating with Japanese communications gear. *Of course, if we get too careless they will figure it out.*

Lt. Ito was now up, and walking into the command center with a new thermos of tea.

Eddie looked at his watch; it was sixteen hours since they had left the cavern.

"Anti-submarine aircraft have made two passes more than an hour apart, and both times they pinged us with a quick series, but then stopped."

"That is strange. The ping should have told them our location," Lt. Ito said.

"Yes, but I think there is a problem with their sonar return because they don't seem to be sure about our location."

"Maybe we should dive deeper and change course?" Lt. Ito said.

"We need more information. It is past two in the afternoon; they should have today's satellite download. Send a signal to

Director K, have him fast burst us the latest satellite report, the East China Sea only."

Again, the command center was filled with the pinging from an anti-submarine aircraft.

"Sir the report is coming in," the radioman said.

Lt. Ito pulled it up on the computer screen and they studied it.

"They're bringing everything this way," Lt. Ito said.

"Send a signal to Director K. Have him fast burst the report for the South China Sea."

Again the command center was filled with the pinging noise from an anti-submarine aircraft.

"Sir, the report is coming in."

They both studied the photo map on the screen.

"They know where we are," Lt. Ito said.

"Yes. They probably knew when their aircraft first pinged us on the second pass this morning. They didn't come back right away because they didn't want to tip us off."

"Lt. Ito, take her down to fifteen hundred feet and increase speed to twenty-five knots. Change heading to nine degrees west."

Eddie studied the map from the South China Sea. The Pacific fleet was sending everything that could float, and placing it between them and the Philippines archipelago.

"It appears they know where we're heading too," Lt. Ito said.

"They don't know what islands yet. But they know the Philippines archipelago is an excellent place for a submarine to hide and they intend to get between the Hercules and the islands.

"Plus they're hoping to trap us between the vessels coming out of the South China Sea and the vessels coming from the east out of the East China Sea," Eddie said.

"And there are a lot of them, and that's just the surface ships," Lt. Ito said.

"Yes, plus the aircraft," Eddie said.

Eddie pushed the button on the map console and then looked at the display—287 nautical miles to destination.

"The American anti-submarine aircraft could probably sink us at any time," Lt. Ito said.

"Yes, but they don't want to sink us—they want the Hercules back."

Eddie and Lt. Ito stood looking down at the map console, then Eddie pointed his finger at the Babuyan Islands.

"At twenty-five knots we can probably get to within ninety miles east of the Babuyan Islands before the Americans have us cut off. They won't let us get closer because they don't want nuclear missiles and the reactor any closer than that to a populated area. In the event they decide to sink us, they won't sink us in the open water unless they think we might escape. If they are unable to trap us with surface vessels, then they will use aircraft with submersible missiles to sink us."

Lt. Ito looked at Admiral Yoshida and could almost feel his despair.

"At least we have drawn the American Navy away from the East China Sea. That has opened the way for Director K to deploy the rest of the stand-alone launchers." Lt. Ito said.

"Already four of the launchers should be in place, and by the end of tomorrow at least two more," Eddie said.

"Let's continue on course, but every hour we will change our heading by less than ten degrees east and then west. Let's keep the Americans wondering what our final destination is.

"If we continue at our current rate it will be within fifty miles of the Babuyan Islands, about three in the morning," Lt. Ito said.

"Good; darkness is to our advantage. Let that be our plan for now. When we get near their blockade, we will let the position of American surface vessels dictate our tactics."

Again, the command center was filled with the pinging from the American anti-submarine aircraft, and it sounded like there was than one.

At three in the morning, they were twenty-five miles southeast of the American Blockade line and seventy-five miles away from the Babuyan Islands.

They turned west and reduced their speed to fifteen knots, and reduced their depth to 1,100 feet, then moved down the line of American surface vessels for two hours. The pinging was constant from surface ships and aircraft.

Eddie was sure the American surface vessels would start moving behind him, and they did, trying to stretch their blockade line farther west.

After two hours, Eddie turned the Hercules, heading due east at twenty-five knots, and at a depth of 1,000 feet. They studied the radar, looking for a gap in the American blockade line. The surface vessels had moved their blockade line west.

Doubling back, they raced towards the longest gap and slipped through the threshold. They ran ten miles towards the islands, but the water became too shallow, and the underwater hills too many. They were forced to reduce the Hercules speed to nine knots and depth to five-hundred feet. They spotted a high hill, and slowly settled on the south side. They now had the hill between them and American blockade line to the west.

"We're within forty miles of the Babuyan Islands. Should we wait until it is nightfall up top?" Lt. Ito said.

"We need to risk downloading an update satellite photo for the South China Sea. We need to know the deposition of the American Fleet. Go to periscope depth and transmit, get the burst, and return to depth." Eddie said.

The signal was sent, and a few minutes later a quick burst was received. Eddie and Lt. Ito studied the reconnaissance photo.

"The vessels from the East China Sea and are going to seal off the end of the islands. This would prevent the Hercules from escaping to the east." Lt. Ito said.

"We're thirty-five nautical miles from the cavern but if we approach any further, the ships coming from the East China Sea will cut us off from an escape to the east. The blockade line has cut us off from an escape to the west. The gap between the islands is far too shallow. They could disable, us with antisubmarine missiles fired from a helicopter, at that depth." Eddie said.

"I think the Americans wanted us to slip through their lines. Now they have us in shallow water and they will trap the Hercules, or sink it. Either way they will recover the Hercules because we will be in a water depth of 6,000 feet or less. That's probably what they have in mind. Let's wait until it's dark up top and make a decision to run for the cavern or escape before it is too late."

Lt. Ito slept for three hours and then brought a thermos of tea into the command center. It was Eddie's turn to sleep.

"If any surface vessels start moving towards us, wake me up."

He slept erratically, as his mind tried to dream of an escape plan. In four hours, it would be dark up top and he had to make a choice. Then he was haunted by the sound of Ensign Crowly's shallow breathing.

Eddie rolled out of the bunk, feeling like he hadn't slept, and more drained than when he first laid down. He poured two cups of tea; Eddie and Lt. Ito studied the map.

"By morning the ships from the East will have the escape to the east cut off. We can't pass through the straits between the islands; it's too shallow. They will disable us with an aircraft launched antisubmarine missile. That's probably what they think we are trying to do—hide around the islands," Eddie said.

Lt. Ito looked at the map of the cavern they were trying to get to.

"This would have worked if we didn't have the American fleet on our ass."

"I think so, too. The plan was to bring the Hercules into the cavern, open her hatches, and let her sink to the bottom of a deep crevice of almost a thousand feet. When the next typhoon was pounding the island, the cavern would be imploded, letting its rocks and debris fall on top of the Hercules, burying the sub forever, or at least a very long time. If the explosion was done discreetly during a severe storm, I think it would have worked."

"And now?" Lt. Ito said.

"Even if we got to the cavern, the Americans would know approximately where we are. Even if we manage to scuttle the Hercules undetected, the Americans would find it in a short time and somehow inspect the Hercules. Then they would know everything."

"Yes, the cavern will no longer work, and we have no place to hide, in this shallow water. Is that why the Americans haven't moved their surface vessels closer to us?" Lt. Ito said.

"Probably, they want to trap us, and they're getting close to doing that. In another hour, it will be dark on top and we need to slip through the gap before the ships from the South China Sea join up with ships from the East China Sea. We lose our last escape route, they will get aggressive and sink us in shallow water."

"What heading?" Lt. Ito said.

"Due east. At thousand feet and twenty-five knots."

"Do you think they will try and sink us when they see we're slipping through their blockade?" Lt. Ito said.

"I don't know, but they don't want us to get through."

Two hours later they left the safety of the ridge, heading due east and parallel to the America blockade line. They turned slightly south and five nautical miles past the last American surface vessel.

They swung due west and increased speed to twenty-five knots, racing into the gap. The last surface ships on the blockade line began moving east at full speed, attempting to close the gap.

The nearest ship from the East China Sea broke formation, racing west, trying to seal the trap but had eight miles to traverse.

"This is going to be very tight."

"Go to maximum speed," Eddie said.

"Should I increase the depth?"

"No, we won't have time to react if we find that we're heading straight for an underwater ridge."

They were half-way through the gap.

Now the command center was filled with a strange noise.

"Sir, what is that?" the radioman said.

"Is that a helicopter?" Lt. Ito said.

"Start zigging and zagging, now," Eddie said.

Eddie grasped hold of the center map console as the sub tilted to the left.

"Hold for three minutes, then go right," Eddie said.

Now another strange noise—but not loud. Again, a loud pinging sound, and the Hercules shook.

"That was a submersible missile fired from a helicopter."

"Dive to twenty-five hundred and right eight degrees," Eddie said.

"There are still a lot of plateaus this close to the islands."

"I hope we don't hit one," Eddie said.

Now another strange noise. The sound grew louder and again the Hercules shook.

"Take her to three-thousand feet."

"Change our heading to fifteen degrees to the southwest."

"Ocean depth is now 9,000 feet," Lt. Ito said.

"Change your heading to due west minus eight degrees. Bring your speed to twenty-five knots."

"That was close," Lt. Ito said.

"That missile was out front and to our right. That was a warning shot. I'm not sure about the second missile. I think they were trying to disable us."

"Another hour, and we will be at 12,000 feet water depth. They don't want to sink us; at that depth, it would be too difficult to recover the Hercules," Lt. Ito said.

"Maintain course, but if we hear a helicopter or aircraft, start zigging and zagging," Eddie said.

Chapter 28

"AT THIS HEADING, in nine hours we will be in ocean depth of almost three miles," Lt. Ito said.

"They will know our heading. Before long anti-submarine aircraft will be tracking us. But they don't know where we are going, or what we're up to."

"Think they will just follow us?"

"Yes, and they don't want to lose us again. If they decide to sink us, then it will be in shallow water because they want to investigate the Hercules. They will probably try to force us into shallow water.

"I want to be over the Mariana Trench as soon as possible, or at least in three miles of ocean depth. If they decided to destroy the Hercules, at least, the wreckage would be at the greatest depth possible. It will take a very long time before they can recover the wreckage of the Hercules, if it is even possible."

"How long before surface vessels are above us again?"

"Approximately ten hours, and probably out of Guam," Eddie said.

White House, Washington, DC

Secretary of Defense Hart and General Meyers stood before President Warde.

"Mr. President, we have found the nuclear submarine Hercules, we currently know its location, we're tracking it, and antisubmarine aircraft are following the Hercules," General Meyers said.

"Will they communicate with you?"

"No, they have not responded to any of our communications. We are continuing to try, but absolutely no response," Secretary Hart said.

"The Hercules was hiding on the ocean floor, waiting us out. They started running out of oxygen and finally started the reactor. When the reactor was started, they knew their signature would be detected, and started making a run for it."

"A run to where?" the President said.

"They headed for the northeast Pacific but veered off during the night. They tried to enter the Philippines archipelago. Our Pacific fleet attempted to trap them in shallow water near the islands. But they escaped our blockade and are now headed due west into the open Pacific. We are not sure what they are up to, but we have them located, and they can't get away, no matter what they do."

"If they attempt to fire a missile, or navigate into a populated area, you need to sink the Hercules. Before we have a disaster on our hands."

"I read you loud and clear, Sir," General Meyers said.

"Secretary Hart, can you stay behind a minute?"

"Hart, what do you make of all this?"

"I'm not sure. It's possible we're overlooking something. I'm going to think real hard about it."

"Do that, Hart, because I have a gut feeling there is more to this than what meets the eye."

Chapter 29

South Pacific Ocean

IN LESS THAN a half hour, they would be over the Mariana Trench. There was now at least one American surface vessel within ten nautical miles of the Hercules. He pushed the button on the intercom and spoke, "We are approximately half-hour away from the Mariana Trench. As soon as we are above the trench, I will set the stern plate at an eight-degree dive angle and all controls in manual operation. All automatic safeties will be disabled. The Hercules will remain at that dive angle until the submarine is crushed."

Eddie paused.

"When you feel the submarine tilt to the new angle of dive; we will have about half an hour to perform the Ritual of Death. I have chosen the Jumonji Giri Ceremony. I am honored to go to my new life with such brave men. May your journey to a new life be swift and peaceful."

"Admiral Yoshida, I would like to stay with the Hercules to the very end. To make sure that everything goes as planned," Lt. Ito said.

"I am honored that you have offered. Lieutenant Ito, the hull of the Hercules will collapse slowly with a lot of noises. The cold water of the sea will start pouring in and you will experience an instant hypothermia, and the dark seawater will begin to drown the life out of you. The walls of the Hercules will start collapsing on you. This is not the way for a samurai to die. You have served Japan honorably. I urge you to die the honorable death of a samurai."

"As commander of the Hercules it is my duty to be the last to leave this submarine."

Lt. Ito knew an order when he heard one.

"Admiral Yoshida, it will be as you wish."

"Lieutenant Ito, unlock the hatch where the American bodies are stored."

He understood. "Yes Admiral Yoshida, I will set their spirits free."

Lt. Ito bowed. "May we meet again in our next life."

Admiral Yoshida bowed. "I would be most honored."

In accordance with the ceremony of Hara-kiri, the crew had prepared a last meal.

"Admiral Yoshida, I have cooked a meal of fried rice, tuna, egg roll, and tea. I apologize for the tuna; it is not fresh, but frozen. The American supplies are lacking in fresh fish," Seaman Ren said.

"I'm sure the meal will be delicious. You are a first-rate cook. I have been honored to serve with you."

"Admiral Yoshida, it is I who has been honored to have served with you."

"Still, I am sorry that your life has to end this way."

"Now, I know how the puzzle of this life will end. We live many lives," Seaman Ren said.

"Yes we do, but I was hoping that you could spend more time in this one."

Seaman Ren smiled.

Seaman Ren bowed in honor. "May we have better fish in our next life."

Admiral Yoshida bowed in appreciation. "May we meet in the next life."

Eddie slowly ate his last meal.

The mystery of how this life would end, he now knew. In his mind and in his heart he felt the sacrifice of his life would save millions; including his wife and children. But still he thought of his first wife and how his life could have been so different. He wondered if his destiny was already decided when he was born.

He placed his death mat on the deck of the control center. Eddie then removed all his clothes. He took water from a bottle and washed his body. Very carefully he dressed himself in his kimono, then he knelt on his death mat. He took out of his bag a Japanese ceremonial paper and pen. In Japanese calligraphy Eddie composed his death poem. He wished he could somehow send his death poem to his wife to let her know—he was at peace.

Now he waited to make sure nothing went wrong. He looked to the back of the passageway leading to the control center and could see some of the crew had already passed on to a new life.

Depth warning alarms were sounding, red warning lights were flashing, and there were strange mechanical noises from the sub. The Hercules had passed its maximum depth rating. The death of the Hercules was proceeding in order. He waited a few minutes; the noises were more frequent and louder.

Solemnly, he recalled The Jumonji Giri Ceremony requires two slashes: one vertical, and one horizontal. Its purpose is to disembowel the intestines, and free the spirit of the Samurai. An honorable Samurai does not cry out in pain as he performs Hara-kiri.

Eddie opened the top of his kimono, picked up the dagger with both hands, and stabbed himself in the abdomen making a vertical incision. The pain was excruciating. He withdrew the blade before his strength diminished and made a horizontal gash. He had disemboweled his intestines and freed his spirit.

He collapsed on his death mat, his life-blood flowing from his body. The pain was gone—his nervous system had shut down—a feeling of peace flooded his mind and spread across his face. Eddie's spirit had been released to the afterlife, and he began his journey to his new life.

Chapter 30

White House, Washington DC

SECRETARY HART AND General Meyers entered the oval office.

"Mr. President, the nuclear submarine Hercules is no longer a problem. Once we detected its location, we followed the Hercules. It ran at its maximum speed of twenty-five knots and tried to outmaneuver and outrun our pursuit. We were able to intercept the Hercules with surface vessels over the Pacific Ocean's deepest depth, the Mariana Trench. The Hercules, already at a depth of fifteen hundred feet, dove deeper and was crushed at approximately four thousand feet. We were never able to establish communication with the Hercules."

"Where is it now?"

"At the bottom of the Mariana Trench—that's approximately 22,000 feet deep. The nuclear reactor has automatic safety systems that disable it in the event of an accident. Everything is safe, just at the bottom of the Pacific."

"Are we going to inform Japan and China?" Secretary Hart said.

"Have our ambassadors in Tokyo and Beijing inform them within the hour that the Hercules has been found at the bottom of the Pacific Ocean. Nothing more."

"Something about this doesn't smell right, Hart."

"I feel the same way, and I don't know what it is, but something isn't right."

Manila, Philippines

General Mendoza watched as CNN announced, "The U.S. submarine the Hercules had malfunctioned during a routine training exercise and now lies on the bottom in a very deep area of the Pacific Ocean."

Chapter 31

Pyongyang, Korea

LI WEI MET with Wang Yong and instructed him to go to North Korea and meet with President-for-life, Jung Yo-han. Express my best wishes for his good health and long reign. Tell Jung, I will greatly appreciate and will be deeply gratified if he can immediately launch a test missile over Japan. Yong straightaway flew in the back seat of a Mig-29 jet fighter trainer to North Korea to meet with President-for-life—Jung.

Jung was delighted to receive an emissary directly from Prime Minister Li Wei, their giant neighbor to the north. It was a chance for Jung to shine. Yong conveyed to Jung the mysterious story of the Japanese paramilitary group and the missing American nuclear submarine.

Further, he explained Prime Minister Li Wei's desire to have North Korea launch a missile over Japan within twenty-four hours. This would test what the Japanese were up to. Jung was eager and wanted to please Prime Minister Li. Jung wanted Li to appreciate his cooperation and feel obligated to return a considerable favor in the future. He told Yong to inform Li that his request would be honored within twenty-four hours.

Without delay, President Jung ordered his chief of staff to prepare to launch a missile, that night, over Tokyo.

"We do not have a reliable missile ready," General Rhie said.

"Use one of the large rockets we designed to put atomic warheads on."

"Sir, they are ready, but untested."

"Not with a warhead; just the rocket. I want it fired over Tokyo, launch time no later than 12:30 tonight. I want to see the light in the sky as it heads to Tokyo before I go to bed. Keep its flight low over Tokyo. Let them see it pass over; I don't want the Japanese to sleep tonight."

"Yes, sir," General Rhie said.

Jung hung up the phone smiling, as he thought about how upset the Japanese and Americans would be. Soon Prime Minister Li Wei would owe him a considerable favor.

Yong encrypted a message to Prime Minister Li Wei. "Jung delighted to accommodate your wishes. Ground crews are now preparing to launch a missile sometime after midnight over Japan."

That morning the North Korea Colonel in charge of the rocket ground crews began barking orders. Immediately crews began scrambling to prepare a rocket for a post-midnight launch. They waited until darkness covered the launching pad, then North Korean ground crews began maneuvering the rocket into position. In the semi-darkness, their rocket preparations would go undetected by American and Japanese spy satellites.

Chapter 32

Pyongyang, Korea

A LITTLE PAST midnight, the North Korean launch pad lit up like daylight. The rocket lifted off and was on its way, and in less than a thousand miles it would pass over the center of Tokyo. Jung put down his glass of shochu, put on his parka, opened the door and walked out onto his balcony, looking southeast into the midnight sky for a trace of light from the outgoing rocket. He could only see a little brightness in the cloud-covered night sky. He felt delighted that the missile launch was on time and the rocket would soon be passing through Tokyo air space.

A few minutes after lift-off, an American surveillance satellite detected the lift off and immediately triggered an alarm that sent a computer-generated message to Air Force Headquarters somewhere in the Rocky Mountains. HQ relayed an encrypted message to Pacific Fleet headquarters. Pacific fleet headquarters encoded a message to the Japanese Defense Forces headquarters. "North Korea has launched a rocket heading for Japan."

A Japanese surveillance satellite had detected the rocket lift off almost two minutes ahead of the US satellite and the Japanese Defense Force headquarters considered the American encrypted message old news. Japanese Defense Forces were already on full alert.

Prime Minister Okada was awakened and informed of the lift-off.

He quickly called National Defense Adviser Sato.

"Why is North Korea doing this?"

"I think the Chinese have put them up to this. They feel we have the American nuclear submarine and are testing us."

"I received a report that Wang Yong, the Chinese military's Chief of Intelligence, flew on a military jet to North Korea, yesterday," Sato said.

"The Americans have reported that the Hercules was crushed as it lost control and dove too deep. I was notified, and so were the Chinese," Okada said.

"I don't think the Chinese believe that. North Korea is a Chinese puppet. Jung would never have launched a missile over Japan, especially Tokyo, without China's consent. I'm sure Prime Minister Li put him up to it. China is ready to make a grab for the islands. They're testing us to determine if we have the will and the ability to defend those islands. I think the Chinese are trying to provoke a response."

He was still talking to Sato when he heard a whining sound and heard an explosion, and he could see the night sky lighting up.

"What is that?"

"Hold on Sato." The Prime Minister walked out on the third story balcony and looked towards a bright light from downtown Tokyo. He saw what looked like an entire street on fire and spreading, as buildings seemed to be exploding into flames.

"Sato, fire is everywhere in central Tokyo."

"Prime Minister, the North Korea rocket hit downtown Tokyo."

As the rocket entered Tokyo air space, Jung lay in bed listening to the rocket-tracking crew relaying its location. It was approaching Tokyo air space when the rocket crew navigator sent a remote encrypted signal to lower the rocket's altitude; the rocket veered towards the ground. The second encoded message tried to adjust its angle, but it only half-corrected. Now it was too late; the rocket was out of altitude. The tracking crew watched, mystified, as the rocket tried to adjust its angle, failed, and plummeted right off the radar screen.

The rocket veered into downtown. It sheered into buildings as it flew horizontally, trying in vain to correct its downward spiral. Fuel sprayed everywhere as it bounced and catapulted along several blocks. Everything it touched exploded into flames; the dry wood buildings particularly ignited with explosive qualities. Fire spread from one wood structure to other wood structures; soon a whole city block was burning, and the fire continued to spread. The rocket came to rest in the middle of an apartment building. The residents who didn't die from the initial impact awakened surrounded by fire.

Chapter 33

Tokyo, Japan

INCREDIBLE;   *ABSOLUTELY UNBELIEVABLE; what the hell was North Korea thinking?* Prime Minister Okada sat on a wood chair in the dark. The flames from a burning downtown reflected off the glass in the balcony doors. He was stunned that it had come to this—central Tokyo in flames, as it had burned in the Second World War.

All the lines on the phone console were blinking, including the American direct line, but he could not bring himself to answer.

He sat there thinking. *Sato is right, the Chinese, and especially Prime Minister Li Wei, were behind this. Li is such a fucking peasant, who in his own stupid peasant mind can't see beyond the Japanese invasion of China, more than seventy-five years ago.*

Li's still fighting the Second World War. How can you live in peace with a man who hates Japan as much as he does? It's a new world order, but not in Li's mind.

If we can't co-exist as peaceful, prosperous countries, then we will have to co-exist in fear of retaliation. A desperate, ugly, frightful way to live, in a balance of horror; the horror of mutual annihilation.

Ignoring all the other phone lines, he picked up the secure outbound-call-only phone, then said, "Sato."

"At your service, Prime Minister."

"We're going to have to strike back."

"What do you have in mind?"

"Sato, you need to advise me; it's your area of expertise. But let me say this, the strike must be decisive, impressive, aggressive and immediate."

"Since the rocket hit Tokyo, I have been thinking of how to retaliate. I know what will strike fear into the Chinese, and give Li Wei a faint heart." Sato outlined his plan.

A little more than three hours later, a Trident-style submersible missile broke the surface of the Sea of Japan, rose high into the sky and streaked towards Northeastern Korea.

More than two hundred miles away and less than a minute later, a second Japanese submersible missile broke the surface of the Sea of Japan, rose high into the sky and streaked towards North Central Korea.

A hundred miles away and a little more than two minutes after the second launch, and scarcely a hundred miles off the Chinese coast in the East China Sea, a submersible missile broke the surface. It rose higher than the other two missiles had, it's nose aimed towards northern China and Beijing.

Chinese coastal defense radar technicians watched in horror as a missile popped up on their radar screens, just off China's shore, and its tracking indicated it was heading north towards Beijing. Its speed continued to increase as its flight-path leveled and it raced towards Beijing; it would strike Beijing within eight minutes.

It appeared to have been launched from the ocean and barely off China's coast. Stunned, they rose from their chairs, their eyes glued to the radar screen, their hands grabbing military alert phones, informing the next echelon. Whose missile it was they were tracking, they didn't know, and where it came from, they weren't sure.

More Chinese radar picked up the missile's flight. Now, in excess of a hundred technicians and military personnel stared in horror at the incoming missile. Their mouths were still hanging open and their minds confused, when the missile's nose slowly turned away from its northern tracery and streaked east towards North Korea. They were only sure that it had to come from the ocean, from a ship, or underwater from a submarine. The way the missile had just popped onto their radar screens was frightening, but the message was clear:*we can strike Beijing before you have time to react.*

The first Trident-style missile traveled in excess of 2,000 miles per hour and was over North Korea in twelve minutes. As the missile turned straight up, an explosion occurred, and the top portion of the shell separated from the main body, and it rose an additional three miles into the atmosphere. This increase in altitude gave its nuclear warheads a smoother glide angle to their targets. As it reached its peak, a second explosion occurred and three nuclear warheads were released. One headed towards the rocket-launching site at Tong Chang-ri. The second nuclear warhead was aimed at the North Korean Air Force fighter base command center at Chunghwa. The third nuclear warhead was headed towards the North Korea Naval base at Haeju.

The second submersible missile streaked into North Korean airspace. Over central North Korea, its nose turned upwards, then rose three miles into the atmosphere. As it reached its peak, an explosion occurred and three nuclear warheads were released. One headed towards the artillery munitions station at Kaesan. The second nuclear warhead spiraled towards the large commando army base at Kaesan. The third nuclear warhead smashed into the large army transportation and food storage facility at Simpyong.

The third submersible missile was just entering North Korean airspace, having traveled more than five-hundred miles from the Chinese coast. As it trekked north of the center of North Korea, it rose three additional miles into the atmosphere and released its payload of three nuclear warheads.

One spiraled towards the military communications center at Sariwon. The second traveled towards the government buildings and President-for-life—Jung's offices in the capital city of Pyongyang. The third nuclear warhead was headed directly at the secret bunker that Jung and his command staff had just scrambled into on the outskirts of Pyongyang. The nuclear warhead hit directly into the thick steel door that Kim and his General Staff had just driven through.

Chapter 34

Beijing, China

PRIME MINISTER LI Wei sat behind his desk. He had dismissed the generals and needed time to think about his meeting with the standing committee of the Politburo. The day had passed, there was no nuclear threat to China, and their nuclear forces were standing down. North Korea was a disaster, he was sure of that. No communications in and no communications out.

He sat in his chair and he reviewed the day's events. Nuclear war had been close, very close. If he had the backing of the Politburo standing committee, he would have wiped Japan off the face of the earth. There would just be water where that fucking island stood. So what if China lost, two or three hundred million people and half a dozen cities? China would survive and Japan would be gone forever, merely a notation at the bottom of a history page, a hundred years from now.

The world was outraged, and the Japanese response was out of proportion to the errant missile that had inadvertently hit Tokyo. He knew why the Japanese had responded the way they had. It was a clear and unmistakable message: *we have nuclear weapons,*

submersible launch capability from anywhere in the South Pacific, and Japan
will strike to protect its territory and vital interests. Despite world opinion.

Li Wei knew he could get by with a nuclear strike on Japan because of
their overreaction to a defective rocket, Japan's blatant breach of the non-nuclear
treaty, their culpability in the Three Gorges dam disaster, and their nuclear
strike on North Korea.

He felt confident that Japan didn't have much more nuclear capability.
Now that the world knows they have been building nuclear weapons, Japan will
not hide its nuclear weapons production. Given time, Japan will have plenty of
nuclear weapons. It would be best to strike now before they are fully capable—
time is on Japan's side.

He stood leaning against the wall, contemplating how many
votes he could get to back his decision to strike back at Japan for
destroying their trusted ally, North Korea. With his own vote, all
he needed was two more votes and it would be three to three, or he
needed one of the oppositions to abstain. He would prefer four
votes, his and three others.

He was still contemplating whom he could swing his way
when his door opened, and in walked the five members of the
Politburo standing committee, and The Whale.

He stood upright; he did not become Prime Minister by being
timid.

"What is the meaning of this?"

"Prime Minister, we have decided to bring the meeting to
your office, here there is more privacy," Wang Lei said.

He looked at their faces and knew they had already made their
decision. He pointed his finger at Zang Tao.

"What is he doing here? He's not a member of the Standing
Committee."

"Because of the events of the last couple of days, the
Politburo as a whole has asked to have a Politburo member present
for this meeting. I think you can understand their concern," Wang
Lei said.

"This is most unusual."

"True, Prime Minister, but this has been a most extraordinary few days. There is grave concern in the entire Politburo. They asked to have a member present to informally advise them as to these proceedings. We all know there is much at stake," Wang Lei said.

Wang Lei had lied but had carried it off well. It helped that the other four members nodded their heads in agreement as he had spoken. He watched Li Wei. He had bought the lie, at least for now. But when this meeting was over, the Prime Minister would be checking the validity of this story.

The Standing Committee stood there, a little hesitant, a little unsure of themselves, a little anxious, and waiting.

Li liked that they were intimidated by his presence. It was time for him to take charge.

"Gentleman, let's get down to business. Now is the time for China to take its rightful place in the world. We are the most populous country in the world. Our economy will soon be the largest in the world. Our military is strong and China fears no one."

He stopped, and considered them carefully. *Who was the weakest? Who could he intimidate? Whose vote could he buy? Who would give in if someone else yielded first? Who needed a favor?*

"What are you saying Li?" Wang Lei said.

This time Li didn't hold back.

"I'm going to strike Japan with punishing blows. They have overreacted in their nuclear strike against North Korea. They have violated their non-nuclear treaty. The Americans will not honor their nuclear umbrella agreement."

He paced slowly back and forth in front of them, his hands behind his back, but his eyes never left their faces.

"We can destroy Japan's military, leave their economy in ruins and their islands uninhabitable, apart from for vermin, and that's what the Japanese race is—rats."

He paused.

"It will also avenge the rape of Nanking, the invasion of our coastal providences that they left in ruins, and the death of millions. The Three Gorges dam, the war reparations that are long overdue to China."

The Whale spoke, his voice, as always, eloquent.

"Prime Minister, you are fighting a war that was over 70 years ago. The only thing that would come from destroying Japan is China would lose a critical customer. They buy lots of our goods, and they pay on time."

Li stopped pacing and looked at Zang Tao.

"Do you know Chinese history? Do you know of the rape of Nanking? Who are you to even talk to me?"

"Li, he should have a voice. He is here with us," Wang Lei said.

The room became awkwardly quiet.

*****

Again the eloquent voice of The Whale broke the tension of silence.

"As for North Korea, instead of selling them our manufactured goods, we will have to send them aid at our expense. If we don't, those cockroaches will be pouring over our border by the millions, and we will have to feed, clothe, and provide medical care for them. And that puts another strain on our treasury. Prime Minister, nothing good has, or will, come of military adventurism. We end up destroying our customers. We sell those economies billions of dollars of our manufactured goods. It's something China excels at—manufacturing. We have cheap labor, thousands of capable manufacturing facilities, and excellent technical knowledge."

Li was further infuriated by the fat man.

"I don't even understand what you are talking about. This is nonsense. Do you even understand what you are saying?"

"Prime Minister, what Zang Tao said makes sense. China has not enjoyed such prosperity in over five hundred years," Wang Lei said.

Li, angrily waved his hand and cut him off.

"I'm not talking about money. I'm talking about China's history, it place in the world, its future, its security, and even its very survival."

Again the eloquent voice of The Whale spoke.

"Prime Minister, it's all about money. The money for your planes, tanks, and ships—this money is derived from our commerce. You need an economy that makes money to support an army, its equipment, food, and payroll. You see, it's all about money.

"The more goods we manufacture and sell, the more money we make, and the more money for your military. But, Prime Minister, we cannot have an army that goes around and destroys our customers. Sir, to say it simply, our customers feed us, and if we destroy them—we will starve."

Li stepped in front of Zang Tao, his hand balled into a fist as if to strike him. Instead, he starting wagging his finger a few inches from his face and shouted.

"Who, I say again, are you, to speak to me?" He paused.

"You are no one! You are merely a fat man, who is a disgrace to the Chinese race." He stepped back.

"You speak of economics; never have you mentioned honor. The honor of the Chinese people, and now the destruction of the North Korean people, must be avenged."

Li walked to his desk and slammed his hand on the desk. The room grew silent.

"The fat one is to leave my office. He should have never been here, and I will get to the bottom of this."

He paused, turned and waved his finger at them. "This is treason!"

No one moved. Li looked at them and could sense their fear—they were scared.

"The fat one will be arrested—as well as the rest of you. Two of you can vote with me, and save yourselves—and your families" Li said.

"Which two will it be?"

Again, no one moved.

He slammed his hand on the intercom button, "Get in here—all of you."

The door opened and he stared, but not at the bodyguards he had expected to see. These men he had never seen before.

"Li," Wang Lei said.

The Prime Minister turned and took a step towards him.

"Li, the Standing Committee has found it necessary to replace you."

Li took another step towards him.

"You do not have the authority to …"

His sentence was cut short. An arm went around his neck as two hands grasped his right arm and a needle plunged into his vein.

Li saw spots in his eyes. As his body began collapsing, it felt like an elephant was standing on his chest. He instantly knew what had happened—betrayal.

The security people placed Li Wei in a wheelchair and pushed him out the door.

They stood there in an awkward silence.

"Li was going to arrest all of us," Li Jun said.

"Sometimes politics can be gruesome," Wang Lei said.

He then took a few steps and stood in front of Zang Tao and looked into his eyes.

"Zang Tao, our committee met in secrecy the last couple of days. We decided if we couldn't resolve our differences with Prime Minister Li, then we must replace him.

"We also voted to appoint a new prime minister and we have selected you. Your philosophy of making China manufacturer to the world has brought prosperity to China. We trust that this thinking will continue to bring prosperity and modern life to the Chinese people. Of course, we must avoid conflicts—conflicts that destroy the customers that feed us."

He paused.

"Tomorrow it will be announced that Prime Minister Li has suffered a disabling stroke. Of course, he had to be replaced as Prime Minister."

The five members of the Standing Committee of the Politburo shook his hand as they walked out of the Prime Minister's office.

Zang Tao walked to the large window of the Prime Minister's office. He stood looking out at Beijing. He tried to grasp his hands behind his back, but they couldn't reach around his bulk. Instead, he placed his hands on his hips. He saw his reflection in the window; he didn't see an obese man, but only a man who could bring great prosperity to China.

Chapter 35

White House, Washington, DC

THE PRESIDENT SAT behind his desk and watched as Secretary Hart and General Meyers read the copies he had made of the "Your Eyes Only" NSA report.

"The Chinese have a new Prime Minister; apparently, Li Wei took ill. This new guy Zang Tao, he's a big one," President Warde said.

"I don't know what to make of all that shuffling in China. You're right; Zang Tao is almost four-hundred pounds. Rumor has it that when he was a businessman he used to love coming to Vegas. They called him The Whale, not because of his size but because he threw so much money around, tens of millions of dollars." Secretary Hart said.

The report was a copy of Japan's Prime Minister Okada Taka's conversations on his top security phone. It was a transcript of conversations between the Prime Minister and Sato Kento, his National Defense adviser.

"The Japanese government was behind the commandeering of the Hercules, those lying bastards," General Meyer said.

"I suppose they weren't after the nuclear submarine Hercules, just the Trident missiles," Secretary Hart said.

"No, not the Tridents. Those missiles they let fly at Korea weren't our Trident missiles, but they sure as hell were probably our nuclear warheads." General Meyers said.

"Yes, they fooled us. It was the nuclear warheads they were after, and they got them," President Warde said.

"Then they put the Hercules in the Mariana Trench where it will never in our lifetime be recovered. So who will ever know for certain?" Secretary Hart said.

"They killed thirty-four of our sailors. What about them?" General Meyer said.

"Yes, what about the sailors? We gotta let that go. People in the military take the same chances we all do when we serve. Unfortunately, they were at the wrong place at the wrong time. The Japanese sacrificed their sailors. Someone was piloting the Hercules when it got crushed in the Mariana Trench."

"Yes, we lost thirty-four boys, but better that than a nuclear exchange where hundreds of millions of lives could have been lost, and untold damage."

"When you think about it, things probably worked out for the best. Now the Japanese are responsible for their security. We are not obligated to defend them with our nuclear umbrella treaty. It's better that way because I don't think I could have convinced the American people we were going to have a nuclear exchange with China over three little Japanese islands," President Warde said.

Manila, Philippines

Now it was time for General Mendoza to fulfill his commitment to Zang Tao to reduce the military threat from the United States. This would allow Zang Tao to cut his defense spending by eighty percent, and use that money to expand the Chinese economy. This would bring employment to millions of peasants, and a modern life. Also, it would allow China the freedom to enter into an Asian alliance.

The next afternoon General Mendoza held a news conference, "The Philippines, Japan, Vietnam, Taiwan and South Korea are exploring a mutual self-defense treaty. China is also being invited to participate."

San Francisco, CA.

Danny Towels stood together with two US senators from the state of California. He had long ago bought and paid for them with campaign contributions; they were his, he owned them, and they would do his bidding. His vote counted.

The senior senator spoke, "There is no need for the US to have a military presence in Southeast Asia, other than Guam. It's too expensive and it smacks of war mongering."

North Korea

The reports were slowly coming out of North Korea. The cities had been spared except for the center of Pyongyang, which had taken a direct nuclear hit. President-for-life—Jung Yo-han and his military staff were nowhere to be found, and it was strongly suspected they might be in the rubble of his secret bunker.

The estimates of dead were around 125,000, mostly military personnel on the bases that were hit with nuclear weapons.

Aid was pouring in from South Korea, Japan, the United States, and several other countries.

The new Prime Minister of China was on CNN News.

"China will send thousands of construction workers, administrators, and medical personnel. We also will send replacement computer equipment, medical supplies, clothing, and thousands of tons of rice, and other commodities. It is imperative that the North Korea economy starts functioning again, and as quickly as possible. There is infrastructure to repair as soon as the roads are passable. China will shift production from some of its factories to facilities in North Korea. We want to bring prosperity to the North Korean people."

Watch for other books by Dennis Porter

U Dead Twice

Building the Money Laundering Biz

20674419R00108

Printed in Great Britain
by Amazon